HELL KAT

HELL KAT

VIVI ANNA

APHRODISIA

APHRODISIA
KENSINGTON BOOKS
http://www.kensingtonbooks.com

ROM
Anna

APHRODISIA BOOKS are published by

Kensington Publishing Corp.
850 Third Avenue
New York, NY 10022

All Kensington Titles, Imprints, and Distributed Lines are available at special quantity discounts for bulk purchases for sales promotions, premiums, fund-raising, and educational or institutional use.

Special book excerpts or customized printings can also be created to fit specific needs. For details, write or phone the office of the Kensington special sales manager: Kensington Publishing Corp., 850 Third Avenue, New York, NY 10022, attn: Special Sales Department, Phone: 1-800-221-2647.

ISBN: 0-7582-1495-2

First Kensington Trade Paperback Printing: April 2006

10 9 8 7 6 5 4 3 2 1

Printed in the United States of America

For Shayla . . . my guiding light

ACKNOWLEDGMENTS

Although my name is the only one on the book cover, I didn't get here alone. I had help. Lots of it.

I want to thank my agent Bob Diforio for putting up with me and all my crazy nuisances that I'm sure drive him nuts, Audrey LaFehr for taking a chance on me, Lisa Renee Jones for all the hard work she's done for me, and for being there when I needed her. To the girls of Allure—Lisa, Sasha, Cathryn, Sylvia, Myla, and Delilah, you ladies rock and I hope you'll share power when we take over the world.

To the managers and staff at Chapters, I thank you for always letting me be me, and for putting up with my brilliant ideas and the fact that I scribbled notes all day instead of working!

And I especially need to thank the most important people of all—my family, who have been there for me from the very beginning when I had no clue what I really wanted to do with my life. And for supporting me when I finally figured it out! I love you more than I can possibly express. Mom, Dad, Lane, Erin, Ryan, Deb, and Shayla . . . you are my pillars of strength, and without you I would not be able to stand.

1

Dust devils whirled viciously around the broken remains of civilization. Buildings that once stood proud and strong were now only jagged cement shards protruding from infertile dirt and rock. The sun was a big glaring ball of light in the sky. Where it had once produced growth and warmth, it now scorched what was left of the Earth with its brutal rays.

Kat looked up into the blistering sun and wondered for the second time today what in the hell she was doing on the outer rim. The fierce, arid wind whipped at her cloak and tried to tear it from her body. Sand peppered her face like a tiny barrage of bullets. Pulling her hood forward, she adjusted her tinted goggles over her eyes and continued to search the rubble for her treasure. No small feat, considering her right eye was covered by a black leather eye patch.

She kicked at the dirt and crumbled concrete with her steel-toed jackboots. Nothing. They'd been searching for nearly two hours now. She glanced over at her partner.

"Damian! See anything?"

Damian stood from where he squatted, raising his head toward Kat, his blue eyes glinting in the sun. He held up his hand, something encased in his glove.

"Just this cute little dolly." He waved it at her, grinning mischievously.

The doll, headless and encrusted in filth, rattled in his hand.

"Quit fucking around. And put on your goggles." Kat shook her head. The kid knew better. An hour under the unprotected sun produced cataracts. Cataracts usually led to blindness. She'd seen it happen more and more. Her sister had succumbed to blindness before she had died from the flu. Damian was lucky he had his hood pulled over his head.

"Yes, Momsie." Damian reached around to his pack and unzipped a compartment. He came away with his tinted goggles.

Kat watched him put them on.

"Better?" He flashed a grin.

She shook her head but smiled. He always managed to make her smile. That was one of the reasons she had bartered for his life three years ago.

He had been an employee of a local junk dealer named Jones. Whipping boy, more like. He did errands for Jones, cleaned up the shop, and, once in a while, loaned out to friends. Loaned, as in pimped out for sexual favors. Men or women, it didn't matter to Jones. He was an equal opportunist. If the price was high enough, Damian could be bought.

When Kat first saw Damian, he was hanging from the ceiling by his hands, his wrists shackled in metal claps. As he was naked, except for a thin strip of cloth hanging over his crotch, Kat couldn't help but notice his long, lean body. Muscles rippled as he twisted side to side, struggling against his restraint. When he managed to turn all the way around, Kat could see the long red welts on his back. She looked down at his dangling feet and saw the instrument of choice lying on the dirt floor: a horsewhip.

Although disgusted by the display, Kat didn't show it. She had a reputation to uphold, and couldn't be seen as soft. It was hard enough just being a woman in these desolate times.

"Selling meat now, Jones?"

Jones had glanced up from inspecting the electronic gadget she had brought him, and eyed Damian. "Caught 'im stealin'. 'E's usually a good boy, but ya can't 'ave the 'elp 'elping 'emselves, now, can ya?"

"I guess not."

Damian met her gaze then. His eyes were as blue and clear as the afternoon sky. High, chiseled cheekbones in a comely face with lips full and sensuous. Pretty like a woman, but—she saw as she gazed down his body—there was no question he was all male. His sculpted chest glistened with sweat.

Jones must have noticed her watching him. "You can 'ave a go at 'im, if you like. Won't even charge ya, since ya're such a good customer."

Kat had wanted a go. She felt the sexual pull. It tugged at her insides, gathering painfully between her legs. Guilt also washed over her as she watched him hang from the ceiling. Scrutinizing his powerful body, she wondered what his skin would feel like under her hand. Wondered what his flesh would taste like if she trailed her tongue over his taut stomach and down lower under the thin cloth. As if privy to her thoughts, he smiled at her, the cloth at his crotch beginning to twitch. She quickly looked away and left the store with her coins.

Two days later she returned with more electronics and bartered for Damian's release. Jones didn't even question her. It was just another transaction to him. They had made a deal, sealed it with a handshake, and she had left the store with Damian in tow. He had thanked her for his freedom.

But several months later, Kat realized he hadn't minded his service for Jones. In fact, some of the things he had to do he really enjoyed. Now he did some of those things for Kat. *Lucky girl*, she thought.

Damian's voice broke into her thoughts. "I think Russell gave us a bum lead."

She looked over at him as he kicked an old metal can her way. It landed at the toe of her boot.

"Yeah, maybe."

Eyeing the dirt and debris on the ground, Kat went over what she knew about the area. It had once been home to a school of some sort. The exact nature of it eluded her, but she knew young children had attended. She also knew that children of old were taught by electronic means. They had access to all sorts of gadgets. It wasn't clear even if they had a teacher. Maybe they had all been plugged into some electronic thingy by wires coming out of their heads.

School. Kat had no concept of what that would have been like. The word and idea were as foreign to her as clean air and fresh water. The little bit of reading and writing she had learned was from her mother before she died. Everything else Kat needed to know she had learned by doing it out on the streets. Not a pleasant education for a young, svelte girl with midnight-black hair and big green eyes.

Russell, another junk dealer, had told her she could find those old learning devices out here. At least a couple of steps above the shit ladder than what Jones had been, Kat didn't mind doing business with Russell. So far he had been honest with her in their dealings. He never tried to skimp on her payment. In fact, he had been feeding her tips as to where certain treasures were located. A win-win situation for them both: she got her money and he got his prize. As far as Kat knew, she was the only hunter he tolerated.

Something glinted in the sun just under a rock pile a few feet away. Moving to it, she bent down and pushed over one of the stones to brush away the earth. A small circle of metal, the size of a coin, lay embedded in the dirt.

"Bring me the pack."

Damian rushed over to where she knelt, placing the bag at her side. She opened it up and took out a large, long-handled tool, somewhat like a paintbrush. With care, she swept at the area around the shiny metal. More metal appeared under the dirt. She took out a small chisel and hammer and chipped around the earth that imprisoned the artifact. She did it gently and expertly, careful not to damage her treasure.

"Is that it?" Damian's velvety voice again broke into her concentration.

"Shut up, will you?" But Kat wasn't asking.

She dug around and under the metal and then set aside the tools and lifted the treasure from the ground. A flat silver disk with tiny buttons on one side lay encrusted in the earth. She rubbed at the metal, clearing away the stubborn, clinging sand. The word PLAY was etched under one button. Kat grinned.

"Is it the music maker?"

"Moneymaker, you mean."

Laughing, Damian wrapped his arms around Kat. He picked her up and swung her around.

"I can just taste the thick, juicy steak I'm going to have. I can almost see the blood on my plate."

"Put me down or you'll see the blood on your face."

Damian did as she said but didn't stop grinning. He eyed her as she put the artifact carefully into the pack.

"Aren't you happy?" he asked.

"I'll be a lot happier after the coins are in my pocket and a bottle of vodka is in my hand."

"You're a lot more than happy after a bottle of vodka." His eye twinkled mischievously.

Kat grinned. "I know." She handed him the pack. "Let's go

before it gets dark. We don't want to be out here much longer. Raiders will come soon." She eyed the surrounding burned-out buildings, looking for any sign of scavengers.

Not the animal kind. The human ones. A few treasure hunters had been killed in this area, their bodies found partially eaten.

They moved quickly toward the motorcycle propped up against a ruined building. Kat glanced up at the first two stories that still stood erect. The rest lay buried under two hundred years of dirt and rock. Often, Kat wondered how any of these structures managed to sustain the damage of the nuclear blasts. The windows were long gone, blown to pieces and melted from the explosive heat. Then the whole place had burned. The fires had raged for more than a year. With no water or rain to extinguish the flames, the fires ate up what was left of the civilized world. If it had been this bad out here, she wondered what remained at ground zero. If anything still stood in the Vanquished City, she'd be surprised.

A shrill call shattered the silence around them as Kat swung her leg over the machine. It was no cry of an animal. At least, not the ones running on four legs.

As Damian mounted the bike behind her, she glanced over his shoulder. Swift, dark movement near a large cement slab confirmed her suspicions.

"We've got company." She kicked the motorcycle over. Thankfully, it roared to life in seconds; sometimes it was not so reliable.

Damian, too, peered over his shoulder. "Fuck."

"Yup. Load my shotgun."

Damian fumbled for the gun strapped to the saddlebags on the bike. "We've got only two shells," he confessed while popping them into the chamber.

"Then pray there are only two of *them*."

"Done," Damian said as he handed her the gun.

"Grab the handlebars." Kat turned around on the seat as if to hug Damian, so she could see their attackers, the shotgun tucked into her side. "Let's rock."

Squeezing the gas, Damian shot the bike forward. It wobbled dangerously to the left, but he soon gained control. Two Raiders dressed in ragged cloaks and dark goggles rushed out at them. Kat kept the gun pointed, but she didn't think she'd need it. The strength of the Raider's legs was no match for the bike's speed. No human could outrun a machine from the past.

"Kat! We have a problem."

Trying to turn her head, Kat couldn't see the danger Damian's wavering voice indicated. "How many?"

"Two."

"Can you go around?"

"No. There's a lot of rock and debris. It's a straight path right to them. If we run into one, the impact might kill him, but we'll go down for sure."

"Are they together or on each side?"

"One on each side."

Kat slid the shotgun into the harness on the bike. Reaching under her cloak, she grabbed two star-shaped steel disks from her belt. They were four inches wide and the blades fit perfectly between her fingers.

"Should we slow down?" Damian asked.

"No, speed up."

Damian turned his head and stared at her. "What? Are you fucking crazy?"

"Are there any concrete slabs near them?"

"Tons."

"Find a good one and take us up."

"You want to jump over them?"

"Yup."

Chuckling, Damian shook his head. "I'm going to get eaten alive by a cannibal."

"No, you won't. I'll shoot you before they get to you." Smiling, Kat raised her arms, tucking her elbows into her body, the throwing stars gripped tightly in her hands.

"That's what I love about you, Kat. You're always looking out for me."

Damian gripped the handle, pulling the gas tight. The back wheel spat up gravel and rocks as he gunned it forward.

"Tell me when we're right over them."

"Okay, hang on!"

As the bike rumbled under her, Kat closed her eyes and muttered an oath under her breath. She would not die out here. There were many adventures she had yet to experience. She hadn't even faced her greatest rival . . . Hades. She couldn't die without first meeting him. How would it look to Hades if she died out here like an amateur on their first hunt? It would give him too much gloating power. She'd never allow that.

Feeling Damian tense, she opened her eyes just as the bike hit a concrete incline. Within seconds, they were airborne.

"Now!" Damian yelled.

Whipping her arms down and back, Kat released the metal stars. Squeals of pain confirmed her lethal aim. As the bike soared overhead, Kat could see the two scavengers, with the steel disks embedded in their foreheads. They slumped to the ground, dead.

The impact of the bike hitting the cement jarred Kat and she knocked heads with Damian. Pain exploded in her ear where she hit. Rocking violently, Damian struggled to keep the bike upright. Clamping her eyes shut, Kat wrapped her arms around him, knowing they were going down.

The front wheel hit a rock just as Damian put on the brakes and turned the handlebar. Instead of flipping over, they skidded to a halt on the side, Damian's right leg pinned under the machine. Finally, they came to a rest against another wedge of cement.

Kat peeked open one eye and turned her head to look at Damian. He had his eyes squeezed shut, but he was grinning.

"Are you hurt?"

He nodded his head. "My leg."

"Then why are you smiling?"

"Because we're still alive."

Kat pushed out from him and rolled onto the ground. "Not for long, if you don't get up. There are two more Raiders running this way." Bending down, she pulled on the bike so Damian could slide his leg from under the twisted steel.

Pain evident on his face, Damian managed to stand. Kat glanced at his thigh. There was a rip in the leather of his pants, and a slow trickle of blood.

"Don't be a baby, it's just a scratch." After righting the bike, she swung her leg over it. "Get on before your blood attracts more of them."

Damian got on behind her and wrapped his arms around her waist. "Okay, but I get hazard pay this time. I need a new pair of leathers."

"You can have a pair of leather underwear for all I care. Let's just go."

Laughing, Damian pressed his lips to Kat's cheek in a smacking kiss. "You're my kind of woman, Hell Kat."

2

Russell was extremely pleased when they arrived with the treasure in hand. Caressing its shiny exterior with just the tips of his fingers, Russell looked like he was in bliss. Kat wasn't concerned with Russell's adoration—she just wanted her money. When he plopped a leather sack of coins in her hand, she felt she'd gotten what she wanted.

After acquiring their money, Kat and Damian wandered to the nearest tavern, feeling hungry and extremely thirsty; hours out in the barren wastelands would do that. They both ordered steak and potatoes, a rare and expensive treat. While society rebuilt from the devastation of the war, unmutated cattle were still in short supply. Kat asked for a bottle of vodka and two shot glasses. They were in celebration mode.

After the server took their order, she furrowed her brow at Kat. "You know, Hell Kat, I thought you were dead."

Kat glanced up at her and smirked. "Hell was full. So I'm back."

Two hours later, after the food had been eaten and the bottle half emptied, Kat felt relaxed and at ease. She was even enjoying the night's entertainment: a striptease by the local prostitute. Damian was also enjoying the show as he danced on the stage, helping Miss Claret out of her garments. The crowd hooted and hollered at them, encouraging them into more than just a striptease.

Kat shook her head as Damian's shirt came flying across the room, landing on their table. Pushing it aside, she picked up her glass and tossed back the contents. The alcohol went down smooth like water, her throat long ago numbed.

As she rubbed a hand over her sharp face and through her sooty black hair, her finger caught in a tangle. Tugging at it, she pulled out a few long strands. Time for a haircut, she thought. It was almost impossible to keep long, healthy hair in this heat and filth. While hunting for treasure, she spent most of her time out on the rims, places where dirt and sand managed to get into all sorts of crevices.

Smoothing back her hair as best she could, she readjusted the string of her eye patch. In the way more times than not, she was almost tempted to go without her patch. But she was vain enough to keep it on. She'd lost her sight in a bar fight. The eye was now blind with a milky white film layering it; a long scar dissected her eyebrow, trailing down her eye and peeking out of her patch just at the tip of her cheekbone. She figured she got away lucky; the man that took her sight was collecting maggots six feet under.

"I see your playmate has left you for the night."

Kat turned to glare at the figure looming over the table. He was six feet and weighed close to three hundred pounds, most of it muscle. He had no neck, and his shoulders were so large they just connected to his head. Kat liked beefy men, but he was too much. She imagined his muscles bulged to compensate for a lack of something else. Thankfully, Kat hadn't experienced the anguish of finding out. It was definitely not for lack of trying on his part. Every time he saw her, he came on to her.

Usually Kat was liberal when it came to sex partners. But Melvin the Muscle was not a pretty man on the outside or on the inside. He was just plain ugly and mean. For excitement between the sheets, Kat didn't mind a little mean in her men, but drew the line at vindictive and cruel. And Melvin was all of the above and worse. She'd seen him break a dog's leg for pissing on the wrong bush.

Kat let her stare go from angry to bored. Hopefully he would get the message. "I allow him his playtime now and then."

"Oh, I like that, Hell Kat." Melvin chuckled as he sat down in the Damian's vacated chair.

"I don't think I asked you to join me."

"Sure you did, baby. I seen the way you look at me."

Sighing, she put her elbows on the table and leaned forward, giving him a direct stare.

"You are a big man, Melvin. It's kind of hard not to look at you."

Melvin grinned, exposing his rotting front teeth. "I'm big where it counts, baby." His hand disappeared under the table. Kat could just imagine what he was doing with it.

Sitting back, Kat rolled her good eye. "Please don't make me vomit a perfectly good steak."

"If steak's what you need, honey, I've got six inches of tube steak just waiting for you."

Kat shook her head in disbelief. Melvin had quite the vocabulary. He gained most of it from his stacks of thin, glossy picture books called magazines, inherited from his dead father. The books contained explicit pictures of naked women, not just unclothed, but legs spread completely open, ass in the air. Kat had had the privilege of being flashed several of these pictures during another one of Melvin's seduction scenarios. He thought the pictures would turn her on. They had, but she hadn't let him know that.

The magazines also had stories in them about the sexual escapades of these women. Kat wasn't sure Melvin could read, so someone, probably his father, had read the stories to him. That was where he got his imaginative vocabulary—pornographic bedtime stories.

"Listen, Melvin, I will never, ever fuck you. So quit wasting my perfectly good night and piss off."

The grin slowly slid off Melvin's face like grease down a frying pan. "Not even a blow job?"

"A what?"

"You know, sucking my dick."

"I will never suck, lick, or touch your dick. I don't even want to see it."

Melvin sat back in his chair. "Oh. Okay, I guess I'll go then."

She'd gotten away unscathed this time. Some nights he wasn't so docile. She'd walked away with a bruise or two during their scuffles. Usually, after one hard knock to the head, Melvin left her alone.

"Hey, Kat, this meathead bothering you?"

Closing her eye, Kat sighed. She opened it and glanced up into Damian's appealing face. Still shirtless, with jeans partially undone, he grinned at her. His thick, dark hair was an unruly mess. Sweaty tendrils curled around his ears. He looked really sexy. It was just too damn bad that that pretty face was going to get wrecked.

Kat swore under her breath. "Everything was fine until you opened your stupid mouth."

Melvin stood, rising to his full six feet. He towered over Damian's lanky frame. Damian blinked up at him, bravado leaking out of his clear blue eyes.

"What did you say, boy?" Melvin clenched his hands into mallet-sized fists.

The crowd in the tavern silenced. All eyes were trained on them.

"Nothing," Damian squeaked.

"He called you a meathead. Which is exactly what you are."

Turning, Damian met Kat's eyes and mouthed, *What the fuck are you doing?*

"Finishing what you started. You know I never walk away from a fight." She picked up the bottle of vodka and took a long pull. "In fact, I think I will even make it worse by saying that Melvin is the biggest piece of shit I have ever met. He's a lying, cheating, conniving asshole that fucks the livestock when no one is looking."

Melvin blushed crimson, but Kat didn't think it was from embarrassment. It was from the rage that boiled beneath his skin. She just hoped that rage was uncontrollable enough for her plan to work.

Damian stared at her, mouth agape. "Well, I think that just about did it."

"Are you sure? How 'bout a drink?"

Damian glanced at the bottle in her hand and then back to her face. She smiled, knowing he understood.

"Good idea." Damian took the bottle she offered. "How 'bout a drink, Mel? No hard feelings?"

"I'm gonna rip off your head and shit down your neck."

"I'll take that as a no."

Damian swiped the bottle across Melvin's head. It shattered into hundreds of pieces. Glass sliced Melvin's face.

Diving under the table, Kat unsheathed a sharp dagger strapped to her thigh and crawled across the floor toward Melvin. She swiftly grabbed his foot and sliced the knife across the back of his leather boot. The leather split like a piece of tender meat and blood erupted from the opening. Kat had cut the tendon above his heel.

Melvin squealed in pain as he dropped to the floor. He grabbed his foot, trying to cradle it in his hands. It was too painful to touch, and he screamed in anguish.

Kat stood up and loomed over him. She almost felt sorry for the pain he was experiencing.

Almost.

Damian stood next to her, the broken bottle still clamped in his hand. His eyes were wide with wonder and excitement.

"Don't mess with me again, Melvin. It won't be your tendon I slice next time, but your balls."

Squeezing his eyes shut as tears streamed down his cheeks, he nodded.

Kat grabbed Damian's arm. "Let's go." She pulled him out of the tavern.

Kat and Damian stumbled back to their place: a large room, in an old gutted warehouse, divided by thin cotton sheets hanging from the ceiling. Because no one wanted to own any long-forgotten dirty buildings inhabited by cockroaches and rats, they lived there free. Sometimes others tried to move in, but the booby-traps Kat had set at the doors and windows kept out most intruders. Occasionally, Kat and Damian came home to the dead or dying, stuck on a spike in the door frame or window-sill.

Both Kat and Damian tumbled onto the old mattress, out of breath from running through the backstreets; they didn't want company following them. Melvin didn't have many friends, but the ones he had were merciless thugs. It wouldn't do to have someone slit their throats in the middle of the night.

"Holy shit!" Damian rolled onto his back, his breath coming in short pants.

Looking down at him, Kat noticed his chest was slick with sweat, and she could almost see his heart pounding in his chest. His cheeks were also flush.

"What's with you?" Kat asked.

"What do you mean?"

Kat glanced at him up and down, noticing the large bulge in his pants. "Your dick's hard."

Damian rubbed a hand over the swelling. "I know." He grinned and wiggled his eyebrows.

"You're a sick puppy." Kat raised herself off the bed.

Damian reached out and seized her arm. "The way you moved, Kat, the way you took him down. I thought I was going to cream my pants just watching. You are one tough bitch."

"And that turns you on?"

"You know it does." He squeezed her arm.

She shook her head. "Save it, Damian. I need a bath."

"I'll wash you."

"How's that?"

Damian sat up and leaned into her, his voice a soft whisper against her ear. "I'll clean you head to toe . . . with my tongue."

Kat reclined and searched his face. His eyes had darkened with lust.

"I'm really dirty."

"I know."

Her body quickened, her insides growing tight at his words. Smiling, Kat leaned back on her elbows.

"Stay just like that." Damian bounced off the bed. "I'll be right back."

He returned with a cloth and a basin of tepid water from their supply. Kneeling at her feet, he took one booted foot in his hands and untied the laces. He slid off the boot and then tossed it over his shoulder.

Kat chuckled. Damian was always playful, but this was new. As he rolled off her sock, she closed her eyes and sighed. He soaked the cloth in the water and brought it up to her foot. He washed her slowly, dragging the sheet between her toes.

She bit down on her lip to stop the giggle that threatened to escape. She was a little ticklish on her feet. But it would be a cold day in hell if she ever giggled. It would ruin her hard-ass reputation.

When she could not feel the wet cloth on her skin, she opened her eyes. Damian had set the rag down in the basin and raised her foot to his mouth. With his eyes trained on her, he inserted her big toe into his mouth. He sucked on it and lolled his tongue around. His wet tongue felt glorious on her neglected flesh.

Damian released her and continued the same ritual with her other foot. By the time he was done licking her instep, Kat was soaking wet from desire. Her insides throbbed exquisitely. Sometimes Damian pissed her off, especially when he acted like a fool. But the man was a master when it came to seduction.

Here was his talent, his art.

Damian set down her foot and reached for the zipper of her leather pants. He undid it and hooked his fingers into the waistband. Kat raised her ass off the bed as he slowly peeled her pants down her legs. He tossed them in the same corner as her socks and boots.

Taking the cloth, he gently wiped the skin on her calves, caressing them as he went. He moved up to her knees and inched his way up her thighs. He circled the rag over her skin, pressing with firm, deft movements.

As he neared her throbbing pussy, she took in a ragged breath. She desperately wanted him to touch her there. To push her over the painful edge on which she was teetering. But he stopped mere inches from the ultimate spot. He looked up at her and smiled, setting the cloth into the basin.

"You're not doing a very good job of cleaning me," she growled.

"No?" Damian raised his eyebrow. He leaned forward and pressed his hot mouth to her shin. "How's this?"

He licked her skin, trailing his tongue in lazy circles. He lapped at her knee and behind it. Kat sighed as he lathed her sensitive skin. Most men knew of only a handful of erogenous zones. Damian knew them all.

Continuing his path to her thighs, he slowly circled the skin, nearing the vee of her body with every breath. He stopped a whisper away.

His hot breath rippled over her sex. Her clit swelled in response. It grew achy and desperate for his touch. Kat closed her eyes and spread her legs in anticipation.

Damian drew back. "Turn over," he growled, his voice low and gruff.

His eyes were dark with passion, and she could clearly see the erection still straining at the fabric of his pants. She turned over and lay on the bed facedown.

Damian nestled between her spread legs. Bending down, he licked at the backs of her thighs, sucking on her muscled flesh and nipping at her playfully.

She inhaled another ragged breath as his teeth sunk into her tender flesh just below her left buttock. His wet tongue moved over her cheeks, trailing seductively on one, then on the other. As he made his way to the valley of her cheeks, she shivered in delight. He stopped at the indentation of her tailbone, moving his tongue up and down.

Kat moaned low in her throat. "Lower, damn you."

"Patience, Kitty Kat."

"I haven't got any."

He chuckled. "I know."

Damian brought up his hands and slowly kneaded her cheeks, spreading them apart. He trailed his tongue down, then up. He lapped at the crevice like a cat would drink cream.

Kat's breathing quickened. The ache in her cunt throbbed painfully. His slow, lazy torture on her intimate flesh was nearly driving her mad. She pushed her ass toward his mouth like a cat stretching toward her owner's hand. Damian dipped his tongue into her, flicking in and out quickly.

With a satisfied smile, she closed her eyes. That was more like it. She moved into him as he pushed at her anus with the tip of his moist tongue. He circled and then licked up to her tailbone.

Pushing her back onto the bed, Damian made a wet trail up her back along her spine. He tugged at her shirt.

"Whoa, boy. You're not done down there." She glanced at him over her shoulder.

Grinning, he continued to pull up her shirt until it was over her head. Damian moved down to her ass and continued his ascent up to her neck to nibble the skin under her hair. While shivers zigzagged down her back, Kat squirmed under him.

"Relax. I'm a trained professional," he whispered into her ear, licking her lobe lavishly. "Turn over."

Kat flipped onto her back, but scowled up at him, wondering what he was up to. He bent down and kissed her frowning mouth, brushing her lips apart. Softening under his mouth, she returned his kiss. She couldn't stay angry with him. He was a giving and inventive lover, always eager to please. She knew he would eventually make his way to where she needed his attention.

Damian always brought her to orgasm. Usually more than once.

He moved from her mouth and pressed kisses on her chin and down her neck. Hands busy squeezing her breasts, Damian circled her nipples with his thumbs, flicking them every so often. Kat groaned and arched her back to push her breasts into his talented hands.

He lapped at her nipples one at a time, teasing them with his lips and teeth. Sucking one into his eager mouth, he lolled it around and gently bit down. As violent sensations surged over her, Kat gasped, but pain quickly turned into pleasure.

Damian continued to nip at her nipples. He moved his hand down her belly, stopping an inch from her sex. Kat moaned and writhed under his touch. Her body tingled and throbbed for release. Her sex was burning up. Desire dripped lustily into the slit of her ass.

He licked down to her flat belly and circled her navel, dipping into it playfully. He scraped his teeth along the sensitive flesh below.

Gasping, she grabbed his hair. "If you don't hurry, I'm going to rip off your tongue and use it myself."

With a chuckle, Damian continued his wet path down to her sex. He hesitated above the soft sprinkling of black hair. She could feel his hot breath over her inner folds. Her clit swelled, reaching out for his touch.

He raised his head and looked up at her face, which she could feel was flushed with excitement. "Oh, yeah, I forgot to tell you—"

"I don't care. Just hurry up and eat me."

He grinned and bent down to part her swollen sex with his tongue. Sliding into her cleft, he flicked at her clit. He nestled down between her spread legs and sucked at her juices as if it were honey.

Her body quickened. She was near orgasm. Bending her legs and spreading them farther apart, she gave Damian full exposure to her sex. He dived in and lapped at her like a dog. With the tip of his tongue, he nuzzled against her clit.

She reached out on the bed to take hold of something. Stretching behind, she gripped the spindles of the brass headboard. She closed her eyes and panted. Her release was near.

Damian mumbled something into her sex.

Her eyes sprang open and she glared down at him. "What?"

He raised his head, his mouth glistening with her lust. "I said Hades is going after the Monolith."

Nearly crushing Damian between her legs, Kat pushed up on her elbows. "How do you know?"

"I heard it from a reliable source at the pub."

"Who?"

"A guy that knows a guy who knows a guy saw Hades in a tavern the village over and said he was asking around for a guide into Van. No one goes into the Vanquished City unless they mean business."

"Doesn't mean it's the Monolith."

Damian cocked a brow. "Do you believe that?"

Kat ran a hand over her sweaty face and let out a ragged breath. She looked down at Damian still kneeling by her legs. Her sex still ached painfully.

"Why in hell are you telling me this now?"

"I don't know. I just thought of it."

"While you were licking my . . . ?"

Damian shrugged.

Reaching over, she grabbed him by the hair. Tugging him forward, she flipped him over and straddled him in two swift movements.

She sneered down at him. "Thank you for the bath, but now it's time to fuck."

She unzipped his pants and pulled them down to his knees.

"Ah, my leg," he whined as the leather from his pants scrapped his bandaged cut.

"Don't be a baby. I have the painkiller right here, if you'd hold still." Gripping his cock in one hand, Kat straddled him and lowered herself. In one swift move, he was embedded deep inside her.

Bending forward, she gripped his shoulders. "You're going to fuck me and then we're going down to see Russell. I will be damned if Hades gets the Monolith first."

Damian reached up and cupped her breasts. "We're going into Van?"

As she moved up and down on his cock, she nodded.

"It'll be dangerous. Very dangerous."

"I've heard the stories. But what could possibly be more dangerous than me?"

Damian laughed and squeezed her breasts as she stroked him up with each movement of her agile body.

Yes, what indeed?

3

"Hades is going after the Monolith. I want to know where it is first." Kat leaned over the cracked linoleum counter and turned her good eye on Russell.

Pushing up his welding goggles, Russell stripped off his heavy canvas gloves and walked over to his workbench to return his torch. "It's too dangerous, Kat."

"Not for me it isn't."

Russell scrutinized her with worry in his doe-brown eyes. "Yes, even for you."

Kat pushed up onto the counter and sat. "Cut the fatherly concern shit and tell me where to go."

Russell shuffled toward the counter. He dragged his left leg behind, a result of having taken a fall years ago and broken his hip. There was no doctor to set it properly, just a local medicine man with his herbs and oils.

"Why do you want it so bad?"

"Because I'm a better hunter than Hades."

"So much anger for a man you've never met."

"I've met his reputation."

Russell turned his haggard face toward Damian, who was squatting on the scuffed wood floor feeding dried meat to Russell's cat. "And what do you think?"

Damian glanced up and grinned. "I think whatever Kat wants me to."

Russell shook his head. "Of course you do." He opened a drawer in the counter and took out a bottle of vodka. "When are you going to get a brain of your own?"

Damian stood. "When Kat gives me one."

Russell chuckled and uncapped the cork to take a long pull.

Leaning forward, Kat plucked the vodka from his hand and took a long drink as well. "Think what the Monolith could do for you, Russell. You'd be the new tech master."

He nodded but didn't make eye contact. "And what would it bring you, Kat?"

She looked out the grimy store window at the dust devils whirling down the desolate dirt street. A young mother pulled her shoeless little girl across the road. They both wore rags; days of dust and grime marked their faces.

"Escape."

She handed him the liquor and he took another long swallow. After wiping his mouth with the back of his hand, he grunted.

"Come, and I will tell you the hell you must enter. But remember," Russell warned, "nothing is as it seems in the Vanquished City."

Early the next morning, Kat and Damian were packed up and ready to embark on their most dangerous treasure hunt to date. They traveled in the early hours of the day since the afternoon brought too much sun and the darkness brought things that only lived in nightmares. Russell told them of a guide that could lead them into the treacherous wastelands of the Vanquished City. The guide resided in the next community—one hundred clicks away.

By motorcycle, they traveled down a road still partially paved toward the guide's location. New growth and vegetation grew out of the cement in some areas, a testament to nature's will. Kat assumed no one had the heart to cut it away. Mother Nature had a way of her own. Moreover, the new people of the Earth did not want to fuck with her again after the devastation she suffered from the nuclear war.

They made the trip in three hours. The village of Burnsbow was not unlike their own community. People hustled about the streets selling their wares and trying to make some sort of living in desperate and desolate days. They found the local tavern and thought it the best place to start. Those who had been to the Vanquished City most likely drank a lot to numb the effects of being in the hellish place.

Since it was still morning, the pub wasn't crowded. A few hard-core customers sat at the bar, and one or two sat in the dark corners nursing empty glasses.

Kat and Damian took stools at the bar, each ordering a shot of vodka. Seeming to be a cautious man, the barkeep tried not to make eye contact with them. When he set their glasses in front of them, Kat touched his hand. His eyes lifted to her face, an expression of surprise in them.

"We're looking for Darquiel."

"Not here," he grunted.

Kat slid a coin across the counter. "When?"

"Later tonight."

When he grabbed the money, she placed her hand on top of his. "Are you sure?"

"Comes in every night. Sleeps all day, then comes here," he retorted as a shiver raked his body.

"I'll give you three more if you tell me where he sleeps."

The barkeep snorted. "Don't know Darquiel if you ask me that." Sliding the dollar coin out from Kat's palm, he dropped it into his pocket and moved away from them down to the end of the bar.

Kat raised her glass in salute to the bartender and tossed back the drink. She looked over at Damian. "Long time till nightfall."

Lifting his lips in a sexy sneer, Damian remarked, "I can think of a few things we could do till then." He moved his fingers up her thigh and in between her legs, rubbing her hard through the leather of her pants.

"Barkeep, is there a place we could rent a room?" Kat growled.

The room was dirty and smelled like week-old sweat and urine, but it had a bed and privacy. That was all they needed.

While Damian stored their gear under the bed, Kat stripped off her cloak, gun holster, and utility belt. Tossing everything on the floor, she grabbed Damian by the hair and pulled him to her. She crushed her mouth to his, overwhelmed with the urge to fuck.

Going on a treasure hunt always got her hot. She loved everything about it—the research, the setup, and, of course, the actual hunting.

Adrenaline surged through her as she nipped his lips and swept her tongue over his. She wanted to play, and she knew Damian was always up for a game. He was usually the one to initiate them, but not now. Now, Kat was in complete control.

Shoving him away, she snarled, "Take off your clothes."

Without hesitation, Damian removed his leather cloak, boots, dark T-shirt, and leather pants and tossed them on the floor next to the gear she had previously discarded. He stood naked and grinning, waiting for her next instruction.

Kat swept her gaze over him, admiring his lean, sinewy form

and his quickly swelling cock. He was pleasant to look at. Tall, dark, and sexy as sin itself. His body never failed to arouse her. And his willingness to do anything she asked made her sex drip with anticipation.

"On your back, boy," she demanded, motioning to the bed.

Damian flopped onto the mattress, spread-eagle. Kat moved to stand at the end of the bed, watching him eagerly. Damian loved to show off. He was an exhibitionist through and through.

"Now get yourself ready. I want you rock hard and aching for me."

With a sly grin, Damian gripped his erection in his right hand and began to stroke himself, with slow and deliberate movements. He was teasing her. She let him have his fun because soon he'd be begging her to end his torment.

While she watched him caress his cock, Kat stripped off her clothes. She kneeled on the bed next to his hip and then smacked his hand.

"Enough. It's my turn."

Chuckling at her playfulness, Damian relinquished his hold on his cock.

"Put your arms over your head," Kat ordered as she took his member in her hand and blew across the tip.

Damian shuddered in response.

"And no touching until I say so," she added.

"Oh, you play a mean game, Pussy Kat." Damian raised his arms above his head and grabbed the metal rods of the headboard. "Oh, what I wouldn't do for a pair of handcuffs."

Kat glanced up at him as she lathed the tip of her tongue across the head of his cock. "Hmm, I have an idea." She jumped off the bed and rummaged through her gear on the floor. She came away with her leather belt. Perfect.

Grinning, she wrapped Damian's wrists together with the belt and then secured them to the posts on the headboard. Damian pretended to protest, but Kat knew he loved it. He had told her about some of the things he was made to do for Jones with some of the people he serviced. One eager woman liked to tie him up and torture him with her tongue.

After securing him tightly, Kat inspected her work. She liked him like this. Defenseless but trusting. Putting his faith in her that she wouldn't hurt him. With his arms stretched over his head, the long, muscular lines of his chest and sides emphasized his slender form, and it definitely did wonders to the positioning of his cock. It seemed bigger, tastier, without anything able to protect it.

"I like you like this," she purred, bending over his groin and flicking her tongue over his fully engorged cock. "All vulnerable and helpless."

Again she flicked her tongue, this time over the dark purple tip. He twitched in response, and a small moan escaped his lips.

"Be nice to me, Kat."

"Hmm," she hummed. "We'll see."

With a low growl, Kat gripped his shaft in her hand and glided her lips over the head. Gathering the moisture beaded there with the tip of her tongue, she swallowed it down, enjoying the salty tang. Gripping his balls in her other hand, Kat opened her mouth wide and took him all in.

He twitched in her mouth as she sucked on him. Bobbing her head up and down, she continued to massage his scrotum, knowing Damian loved it. His balls were hard and tight, and she knew he was close to climaxing. But she wasn't ready for him to come just yet.

Tightening her grip at the base of his shaft, Kat squeezed him off. She brought up her head and lavished her tongue over the tip and down the underside of his glans where she knew he was the most sensitive.

"Ah, Kat, fuck, you're killing me." Damian writhed and pulled on his restraints.

"No dying just yet. I'm not nearly done with you."

Still stroking his cock, Kat turned and swung her leg over Damian's stomach so that her ass was facing him. Carefully, she shuffled backward to hover deliciously over his face.

"Mmm," he moaned. "This would be better if I had hands."

"I'm confident that you'll do just fine without them." Slowly, she lowered herself down to him. She could feel his hot breath on the soft folds of her sex. Already, she was wet and open, anticipating his eager tongue inside her.

Spread wide and bare over his head, she felt the tip of his tongue sliding along her cleft. Sighing, Kat inched down closer, forcing her legs farther apart, urging him for more. Damian could do remarkable things with his long, wet appendage.

Leaning forward, Kat wrapped her lips around his cock, sucking him in eagerly. As she did, Damian lapped at her slit, swirling his tongue around her opening and then back up to her clit. He flicked it back and forth and then glided down to her opening.

As Kat bobbed her head up and down on his cock, she could feel a hard orgasm building like a fuse on a bomb. With its sizzling and slowly making its way to the climax, she knew it would be explosive. Orgasms were great tension releasers. And Damian always gave her good ones.

Kat found it hard to concentrate as Damian swirled his tongue into her pussy. He pressed and inched his way in, slurping on her intimate flesh as he went. She pushed down on him, imploring him to go faster, go deeper.

As he darted his tongue in and out of her, Kat slid his cock into her mouth to the base and sucked on him hard. His balls, gripped in her hand, clenched and tightened. It wouldn't be long before he orgasmed, too. But she wanted to be first.

Sitting up, she buried his face into her cunt, thrusting her hips back and forth. Damian took the cue and covered her clit with his mouth, sucking on her hard. Closing her eyes, Kat moaned as her orgasm started to surge over her. It started deep in her belly and rippled outward through her pussy.

After one final flick of his tongue on her aching nub, Kat fell forward as explosive sensations radiated out from between her legs. The orgasm slammed into her gut and overpowered her with its tight, scorching grip.

Unable to think, she could only feel as flow after hot flow of pleasure washed over her and drowned her in its sweet, wet embrace.

Wanting Damian to experience the same ecstasy, she leaned forward and glided her mouth over his cock. Squeezing his balls, she stroked him quickly with her lips, rubbing his flesh with her fingers at the base of his shaft.

His tongue disappeared from her slit and she could feel his hot pants of breath as he struggled to hold his climax in check. Increasing the pressure of her hand and the speed of her mouth, she stroked him hard as her own orgasm quieted.

His balls twitched under her grip. Damian couldn't keep his orgasm at bay any longer. With a loud groan, he emptied himself into her mouth.

"Ah, fuck!"

His legs twitched, and he pulled hard on his binding as she sucked him dry. She could feel him struggling, and with one final yank of his arms, she heard her belt snap as it came undone.

"I'm going to eat you alive, woman."

Damian wrapped his arms around her hips and brought her down to his face. She could feel him nuzzling into her sex, and fresh hot desire flowed through her. Letting his flaccid cock slip from her mouth, Kat sat up with her hands braced on his stomach and settled in for another explosive orgasm.

Pulling her nether lips apart with his thumbs, Damian slid his tongue into her again. Still sensitive from the last orgasm,

Kat knew it wouldn't take much to push her over the edge. Already, she could feel tiny jolts of pleasure zigzagging over her body.

As his tongue slid in and out of her, Kat could feel his fingers beginning to explore. She sucked in air as Damian swirled his finger past her opening and up to her anus. With the moisture of her past orgasm on his skin, he easily slid into her.

Her thighs tightened instantly as a sizzling crack of pleasure whipped over her. She could hardly catch her breath as he pumped his finger in and out of her ass and slid his tongue up to her clit. She flinched the moment he touched her aching pearl. Still tender and throbbing, she had to grit her teeth to stop from screaming. She wanted to scramble away from the conflicting jolts of rapture and pain stabbing at her, but Damian held her down with his palms on her thighs.

"Ah, Jesus!" She couldn't stop the groan as he slid another slick finger into her anus.

As he thrusted in and out, he covered her clit with his mouth. Pressing around it with his lips, he began to roll it back and forth.

Instantly, Kat felt an explosion inside her. White light flashed behind her eyes and she screamed, losing her breath with the impact of the orgasm. Damian continued his assault on her flesh. Wave after wave of ecstasy smashed into her. All thought escaped her, and she collapsed onto Damian, unable to hold herself up on her quivering arms.

Slowly reason returned to Kat as her climax quieted and her body stopped quaking. Feeling Damian's labored breaths beneath her, she rolled off him and onto the mattress. She pushed up onto her elbows and looked at him.

His eyes were closed and he had a grin of pure satisfaction on his face. His lips glistened with her lust.

"You win," Kat said and then yawned as her lids grew heavy.

"I didn't know we were playing a game."

"Honey, we're always playing a game."

Damian pried open one eye. "Okay. Now, what's my prize?"

Yawning again, Kat laid back down. "Five hours of uninterrupted sleep."

As she gathered the blanket on the bed and pulled it over her like a cocoon, his chuckle was the last thing she heard.

4

When darkness settled in, Kat and Damian returned to the little tavern. Business had picked up. Now all ten tables were occupied and every stool at the bar was taken. Some people stood at the counter, leaning on it for comfort and support.

Heads turned when they walked in. Two people dressed in black leather, as they were dressed, always meant trouble. Treasure hunters were not well liked. Some frowned on their pursuit of profit, even calling them thieves. Kat liked to think of herself as an archaeologist, bringing the past to the present to ensure her place in the future. It was all a matter of supply and demand.

They sauntered up to the bar. Two patrons made room for them, squeezing closer to their neighbors. Kat slid some coins onto the counter. The same barkeep from the afternoon eyed them, reluctance swimming in his dung-brown eyes.

"Three vodka shots and you-know-who."

The barkeep poured their drinks and took the money. "In the corner," he said under his breath.

Picking up their drinks, Kat and Damian turned around and scanned the room. Kat's eyes rested on a dark corner. A lone patron sat at a table, slumped forward, a half-empty glass in the middle of the worn, scarred surface.

Kat headed toward the table.

"Can we join you?" Kat asked, eyeing the empty seats.

No answer. Not even a movement. All she could see were bone-white spiky hair and motionless, thin, pale hands resting on the wood. Kat and Damian sat down on either side of the table, surrounding the silent individual.

"Thought you could use a drink." Kat set a drink by the stranger's hand, keeping one for her own consumption.

Abruptly, the head lifted, revealing a gaunt face so pale that blue capillaries showed underneath. Surprise caused Kat to lean back in her chair. Damian jolted, his vodka sloshing over the rim of his glass.

The girl's eyes were a color so dark that they blended into one complete black circle. Full lips that might have been attractive were dry, cracked, and colorless. She appeared to be the ghost of a woman who had once been considered dainty and ethereal.

"Do I look like I need a drink?" Her voice was soft and quiet, barely audible over the din of the crowd in the tavern.

"Yes." Damian spoke before Kat could open her mouth.

The girl turned, fixing him in a dark stare.

Damian blushed. A thing Kat didn't think possible.

"Are you Darquiel?" Kat asked.

The girl turned to Kat and picked up the vodka shot, tossing it back in one gulp. "Darquiel is the angel of peace and understanding. I am no such thing."

Kat smirked and set a small leather pouch on the table. "We are in need of a guide into Van. We were told you would be of service."

"You were misinformed."

Kat upended the pouch onto the table. Gold and silver coins spilled out. "Are you sure?"

Darquiel never looked away from Kat. "No amount of money could make me go back."

A large shadow enshrouded them. A black leather pouch plopped onto the table. "How about that much?"

Kat didn't need to peek behind her to know who had joined them. She had been expecting him, and was surprised it took him so long.

"You're too late, Hades. She already agreed to an arrangement."

Kat turned in her chair to glance up at him. A twinge flared in her gut as she examined him. He was more than she expected. She knew he would be tall and wide, but that was an underestimation. Easily 6'3" with broad shoulders, Kat bet he had to come in sideways through the door. He was muscular like Melvin the Muscle but not as bulky. He had a neck at least.

"Nice try, honey, but I don't think so." He winked.

The twinge flared again. This time it was a little lower. He had a sexy smile, an even sexier dimple in his cheek, and nice straight teeth. Rare things these days. But it was his eyes that ignited her fire. They were so blue it hurt to gaze upon them. Like peering into the hottest part of a flame. Framing them were impossibly long, dark eyelashes. His head was completely shaved, and a long white scar curved down from the crown of his head to just above his right eye.

Kat found that extremely erotic.

Standing up, she stepped in close to him. "Did you just call me honey?"

In a slow, thorough perusal, Hades did nothing to hide his obvious approval of her body. "You know, Hell Kat, you're not as ugly as I thought you'd be."

She smirked and cocked her eyebrow. "And I thought you'd be bigger."

They stood toe-to-toe like boxers across a ring, gauging each other, searching for weaknesses.

By the way Hades gawked at her, Kat imagined he was drinking in his fill of her long, firm legs and round ass molded seductively in her leather pants. Kat knew he liked what he saw. Her cloak was long and covered most of her, but she was sure he caught a glimpse of ample cleavage. Someone once told her she had been built for sex. That her midnight hair was meant for pulling, and her full ruby lips for kissing. By the glossy mien in his eyes, she assumed that was exactly what he was thinking. Too bad she'd have to disappoint him. The last thing she was going to do was give him the satisfaction of finding out how true those statements were.

Darquiel bristled in her chair breaking the spell. "I never agreed to anything."

Damian set a hand on Darquiel's arm and patted her. "Don't waste your breath. They're not listening." He downed the rest of his drink. "Besides, it's not about you anymore."

Darquiel studied Kat and Hades. "They're not going to fight, are they?"

"Most likely," Damian answered.

"But he'll pulverize her," she sputtered.

Damian chuckled. "Not my Hell Kat, he won't. He may be big, but she's a whole lot of mean and nasty."

"What do you say, Hades, I'll flip *you* for her?" Kat pursed her lips in a sexy pout.

"How 'bout I flip you for her? I don't think you could lift me."

Kat laughed. He was a cheeky bastard. But she did notice the effect she was having on him. Was that a bulge in his pants as he shifted his stance?

While his eyes did another broad sweep of her female form, she took advantage and drew her blade, pressing it to Hades's throat before he had time to blink.

The crowd in the bar fell into a quiet hush. With them perched on the edge of their seats, Kat imagined each secretly wished for bloodshed.

"Concede and I will let you live," Kat demanded, her hand sure and steady at his neck.

"Are you kidding? I'm having too much fun."

Hades grabbed her arm, twisting her around so he that pressed into her back. Her knife arm was pulled tightly against her stomach, and his other arm was snug around her neck.

Kat swore under her breath. She hadn't anticipated the move. Her mind was clouded by too many pheromones. The throb at her center intensified as she felt his hot breath on her ear.

"Concede and I will let you leave with your," he paused to nuzzle against her ear, "honor still intact."

The rigidness of his erection pressed into the small of her back. It felt as hard and big as the rest of him. To stop the groan that wanted so desperately to escape her throat, Kat bit down on her lip.

"You arrogant bastard!" she stammered through clenched teeth. "I'd sooner fuck a dead Raider!"

Hades chuckled gruffly. "I love it when you say 'fuck.'"

Darquiel leaned over to Damian. "She's done now."

"Nope. She's just getting started."

"You like that?" Kat teased.

"Oh, yeah," Hades groaned.

"You like this, too?" Kat pushed her ass into his crotch and moved slightly, rubbing against him.

Kat could tell by the way he grit his teeth that he was suppressing a moan of pleasure. What he failed to say with words, she could hear in the way his body responded to her. Poor sap. He didn't stand a chance.

"Of course. Who wouldn't?" He tried to make his voice sound casual, but she heard the strain.

"Well, enjoy it," she hissed, "because this is the last time you'll ever have my body touching yours."

He bent his head down and blew across her neck. "Well, now, Hell Kat," he crooned, "you don't really mean that, do you?"

Her body stiffened at the intimate contact. She was just as responsive to him as he was to her. Damn hormones! But she wasn't going to let the fact that she thought about lying beneath him, her legs wrapped around his waist, defeat her main agenda. She would show Hades she was not some tart he could play with.

Taking a deep breath, Kat jammed the heel of her boot into his shin. With her other hand she reached high over her head and grabbed him around the neck. She pushed back and bent forward.

Kat didn't know if the move would work. But he had his height against him. All she had to do was set it in motion. As she considered him, sprawled on the hard tavern floor, she thought the pain in her spine was well worth it. She slung the sawed-off shotgun forward from where it had been hanging inconspicuously around her shoulder.

She cocked it and pointed it at Hades's shocked face. "Are we done?"

Hades stared up at her and into the barrel of her shotgun. She wanted to laugh at the shock on his face. He was probably asking himself how he could have missed seeing the weapon on her. Most likely he had been thinking with his cock and not his head when he assessed her and failed to spot the shotgun cleverly concealed under her cloak.

"Okay. I'll share the prize with you," he offered.

"What?" Kat shook in head. He couldn't be serious. Then again she supposed that if he gave up so easily, he wouldn't have the reputation he had. She heard that he never walked away from a treasure hunt.

"We split the cost of paying the guide, and we split the treasure," he suggested.

"I don't play well with others."

Hades motioned toward Damian, who was now standing, excitement flushing his face. "What about him?"

"He's different," Kat stammered.

"I could be different, too." He gave her a half-cocked smile, that sexy dimple winking at her.

Kat had to resist the urge to smile in return. Damn the insufferable bastard, he was just too sexy.

"I don't think so."

"Okay. Think about this," Hades offered. "There's going to be a lot of others out there looking for the same thing. Others who aren't as cordial as I am. I would be mighty helpful in a fight."

"I can look after myself."

"Granted. But it will be hard to protect a guide, a partner, and the treasure all by yourself."

Kat had considered the possibility already and was trying hard not to think about it. She didn't want to believe that anyone on this trip was expendable. But the reality of it was that someone might be. And she didn't want to delve into that likelihood. The thought was far too frightening to her conscience.

Sighing, Kat flicked on the safety on the gun and let it fall to her side. "We go by my rules or you can forget it."

Hades sat up and brushed the dirt off his leather coat. Standing, he swept at his pants. "Sure, whatever, babe."

"Rule number one: No 'babe,' 'honey,' 'sweetheart,' or anything else related to gender. And no sexual innuendoes."

"Damn, you might as well just rip out my tongue."

Kat shot him a nasty look. "Is that a request?"

In answer, he bowed arrogantly, his arm swept to one side.

Damian grabbed her arm and pulled her toward him. "You're

not serious?" He spoke quietly into her ear. "He'll kill us all after we get the treasure."

"It's a chance we'll have to take. We need him to ward off the other scavengers and worse things we'll find in the city."

Damian searched her face. "You're not attracted to him, are you?"

"No." She yanked her arm free. "He's repulsive."

"I know you, Kat, and the flush on your face is not from anger."

Kat peered into his eyes. "Damian, if you have a problem, you can stay here. I'll still share the bounty. If you're afraid . . ."

"I'm not afraid."

"You should be." Everyone turned toward Darquiel. She sat in her chair, staring out, but not at anything they could see. "I will not go back. Your fight over me was for nothing."

Kat raised both leather sacks. "You'll have enough money."

"Your money cannot take away my pain."

"I could ease it with a bullet." She raised her shotgun, pointing it at Darquiel.

Darquiel turned and gazed at Kat, her eyes black and lifeless. "There are more frightening things than death, and I have seen them."

Kat saw the pain and suffering etched in Darquiel's pale face. Obviously the girl had seen too much, experienced things too agonizing to explain. Kat dropped the gun and took her leather sack, emptying a few coins on the table.

"I'm sorry for your pain, but I am going into Van with or without you." Kat tied her pouch and slipped it into her cloak. "Those are for your trouble."

She grabbed Hades's pouch and tossed it to him. "Looks like the deal's off. First one to the Monolith wins."

Hades caught it and tucked it into his jacket. "It'd still be better if we go as a team."

"Why? Are you afraid, too?"

"No, but I'm cautious. As you should be."

"Fuck caution. I wouldn't be a hunter if I was cautious, and the Hades I learned to respectfully despise isn't either." Kat turned on her heel to leave. "C'mon, Damian."

Damian hesitated, glancing down at Darquiel. She regarded him with longing on her strained face.

"I'm going to stay for another drink."

Kat turned and glared at him. She glanced down at Darquiel, then back at him, and sniffed. "Suit yourself, but we're leaving at dawn. So be ready."

Before she could make her escape, Hades grabbed her by the shoulder. "The Hell Kat I heard about is not a fool. Why are you acting like one now?"

"Excuse me?"

"The Vanquished City is not the Outer Rims. It is nothing either of us has faced before."

"I never thought you, of all people, would listen to fairy tales designed to frighten children."

Darquiel stood up. "They're not stories."

"Look," Kat acknowledged, "I don't deny your pain and suffering, but I refuse to believe it was at the hands of something otherworldly. I don't believe in ghosts or ghouls."

"Your disbelief does not make them less real," Darquiel declared.

Kat looked up at Hades, her brow cocked. "Don't tell me you believe in the bogeyman?"

"Not the bogeyman, Kat. But think about it. Van City is at ground zero. Who knows what the radiation has done to the animals," Hades paused, and then added, "and people over the past two hundred years."

"Fine." She scanned the three faces. Looks of worry and apprehension filled them. "Meet me here, outside, at dawn. No later."

Hades let go of her arm, nodding his assent.

Kat glanced at Damian one last time. He did not meet her gaze. She turned and walked out of the tavern, not allowing the hurt of his refusal to join her to worm its way into her heart.

5

Kat stirred at the first signs of dawn. The early morning glow peeked through the grime and dirt of the hotel room's cracked window. Stretching, she turned over to wake Damian.

The bed was empty and cold.

Sitting up, she looked around the small, cramped room. Damian was busy in the corner, shoving worn clothes into his pack.

"Did you just get in?"

Damian didn't peer back at her, but nodded slightly.

"Did you sleep?"

"No."

Throwing off the bedcovers, Kat extended her arms over her head. "Eat some coffee beans. You'll need the buzz to keep up."

Damian stopped his packing and stared at her as she stretched her back and legs. His look of contempt spoke volumes to her.

"What?" Kat questioned.

"Nothing." He turned away.

She straightened and grabbed her pack. "If you want me to be mad, I won't. You're a big boy. I don't own you."

"Don't you?"

Glancing up, she met his gaze. Something had changed in his eyes. After taking out a fresh shirt from her pack, she stripped, talking while she pulled the new cotton over her head. "Maybe at one time. But you worked off your debt to me. You've been free to leave for a long time."

Grabbing the water flask, she took a big gulp, gargling it and then swallowing. She turned and studied Damian in earnest. He seemed lost and guilt-ridden. "Is that what you want? To leave?"

Damian shook his head. "No."

"Then this conversation is pointless. Hurry and finish. I refuse to be late."

She eyed him as he continued to shove his gear into his bag. Something had changed. Something in him. It wasn't an obvious physical change. Not anything a person could point out just by glancing at him.

But Kat could see a difference. The carefree look in his eye was gone. And she wasn't quite sure what it was that had replaced it.

As Kat and Damian approached the tavern, Kat spied Hades leaning casually on his motorcycle, smoking a cigar. She also noticed that the bike was bigger than hers was and packed well with supplies.

She pulled up the bike next to his and stopped. "Nice ride. Must have cost you."

Hades winked. "Who says I paid for it?" He straddled the machine and kicked it over. The engine roared to life. "We should ride till midday and then find shade to eat and rest."

Kat nodded. No point in arguing . . . yet. The same thoughts had crossed her mind. It was smart and logical. Kat revved the engine and pulled it forward.

"Wait!" Damian yelled over the clamor.

Kat peered beyond her shoulder at him. "For what?"

"For me." From around the tavern's corner, Darquiel appeared, dressed in a long, gray cloak. The hood covered her head and she wore tinted sun goggles to protect her eyes. A small pack hung over her shoulder.

"What do you want?" Kat demanded.

"I'll guide you to a safe place to enter the city. I would hate to see you fall into the wrong hands." She glanced at Damian as she spoke.

Kat eyed Hades. Shrugging, Hades held out his hand to Darquiel. "Get on."

Before hopping onto his bike, Darquiel strapped her bag onto her back. Jumping onto the seat, she wrapped her arms around Hades's waist. Kat thought she appeared to be like a little, pale, porcelain dolly behind his massive form. She wondered if the girl would be an asset or a liability. As they could not afford any liabilities on this trip, she hoped desperately for the former.

After five hours of driving down a depleted road full of holes and fallen timber, they pulled off near a meager, trickling stream of water and a clump of tall trees. The trees would provide the much needed shade, and the stream much needed water.

Kat rubbed her ass after she dismounted the bike. The ride had been bumpy, to say the least. Around the third hour, her left cheek had gone numb.

Hades parked his bike beside hers, watching as she rubbed her rear end. She glared at him.

"Want me to do that?"

"Fat chance in hell of that happening." Kat unstrapped her

bag from the bike and carried it to a shady spot on the yellowing grass beneath an oak tree. She took out her water canteen and drank greedily from it. Sweat already trickled down her back and the sun was not yet at its zenith.

Hades helped Darquiel off his bike. She stumbled slightly and he had to right her.

"What's with her?" Kat asked.

Rushing to her aid, Damian helped Darquiel to a shaded spot on the ground. "She's not usually out in the sun. It makes her sick." Damian pulled down her hood and laid her on the grass. Her face glistened, sickly with sweat. Kat handed him the canteen. He put it to her lips and she drank.

Kat watched her, caution ringing a few bells in her mind. "Is she sick? Does she have some disease?"

"Not a disease. It's like she's allergic to the sun's rays." Damian stroked her hair like a parent with a child or a lover with his mate.

Uneasiness twisted her gut as Kat watched him soothe her. "Did she tell you how she got like this?"

Damian shook his head and continued to stroke Darquiel's white hair.

"Just don't let her drink all the water."

Damian glared at her. "You're really cold, you know?"

"Oh, please, Damian, don't tell me you just figured that out."

Kat walked away and followed the trail down to the little stream. Kneeling, she cupped the fresh water in her hands and took a little sip. It was cool and tasted untainted. Of course, she couldn't be absolutely sure. Some poisons had no taste. She splashed the rest over her face and neck.

A black boot came into her frame of vision. She glanced up while Hades wrapped a white kerchief around his head.

"What do you think?" he asked.

She stood up and rubbed her wet hands on her shirt. "I think she'll be more trouble than she's worth."

"Maybe." He bent down and splashed water over his face and head.

"I'm sorry, Hades, I just can't believe in ghoulies. She must have been born that way."

He picked up a rock and skipped it across the water. "Radiation can do a lot of damage. Mutations are normal. You know that. It's just been in the last twenty years that the cattle have been normal. When I was a kid I saw a cow give birth to a two-headed calf."

She chuckled. "Did you get to name it?"

He stood up and wiped at his face. "I didn't get a chance. It went nuts and tried to tear me apart." He turned over his arm. A long, white scar dissected his forearm, from elbow to wrist. "It also had fangs. I had to stab it in the throat with a stick before it ripped me apart."

"How old were you?"

"Nine."

Kat looked from his injury to his face to study him for a moment. There was more to him than she realized. More than she wanted to imagine. The thought made her uncomfortable and she dropped her gaze to stare across the stream.

"Sorry."

"For what?"

"That you didn't get a chance to have a two-headed cow as a pet."

Hades chuckled. "Yeah, that would have been cool."

"We should go back and eat and then rest. We've got at least six good hours left on the road before we stop to camp."

Before she could ascend the hill, Hades touched her arm to halt her movement. "We have to talk about the possibilities. We need to be prepared for anything."

"I know." And that fact caused shivers of dread to race down her spine. There was more than treasure waiting for them in the dark of the Vanquished City.

* * *

Hades watched as she scrambled up the embankment. She was a tough and disciplined woman. Her reputation as a hunter was unparalleled—even with his own. But behind all that bravado, Hades could still see the fear, the uncertainty. It was the same feeling he had. That the point they were so desperately trying to get to might be the one place they all secretly feared. Hell itself.

He never expected to hook up with Kat when he walked into that bar in Burnsbow. His intentions had been to outbid her offer of payment, steal the guide from her, and eventually get the big score. She had taken him by surprise. He didn't expect to see a woman like her, with darkly sexy looks and a killer body. Nor did he expect to be completely stunned by everything about her. No woman had had that effect on him before. He was quickly learning that Hell Kat was not just any woman.

Kat glared down at Darquiel as she slept. The girl's face twitched erratically, and she moaned as if in pain. Damian sat beside her and stroked her hair.

"We should leave her," Kat prompted. "She's too much of a liability."

Damian jumped to his feet. "You want to leave her here? She'll die."

"She'll endanger us all. We could all die because of her . . . her fragility."

"It's not a flaw, Kat. She can't help the way she is."

"It *is* a flaw. A detrimental one. There's no room in this world for weakness, Damian. You of all people should realize that." Kat regretted the words even before they came spewing out.

Damian flinched. "You're right, Kat, as usual. But if it were not for *my weakness*, who would you have at your command? No one. My weakness ensures your strength. Remember that."

Pain flashed across Damian's pale, angular, face. She hadn't meant to hurt him. He'd been nothing but loyal to her. A lover and a friend. He didn't deserve her cold appraisal. Neither did the frail, sickly girl groaning at his feet. But she could not allow them to jeopardize the mission.

The Monolith was her link to the freedom she craved. The freedom to escape the desolate wastelands and find her way north to a cleaner, more sanitized way of life. A place where she could settle down in a little cabin in the middle of forgotten land. Where disease and violence had, long ago, evaporated in the cool fresh air of a land reborn. But this dream cost money. And the Monolith would grant her those riches.

Damian sat back down beside Darquiel and continued to caress her sweaty brow. As he murmured soft words to her, her face calmed and her twitching ceased.

"If you leave her, I'm staying, too," Damian stammered.

Watching him with Darquiel produced a strange twinge in Kat's gut. *Was this jealousy?* Damian had never touched her like that. Never murmured soft words or touched her with such tenderness. She supposed she had never let him. Her brick walls were erected high and thick. No one had ever gotten in.

"Fine. Keep your pet. But she's your responsibility."

Kat picked up her pack and found another spot in which to hunker down in the shade, away from Damian, distancing herself as she always did. Before they continued on their journey, she would require rest. She suspected that she was going to need all her wits and strength if she was going to survive this hunt.

6

After rest and food, Kat and Hades drove for another six hours, stopping only for water and small bits of dried meat. When the sun went down, they pulled off the road and made camp for the night against a couple of large, jagged boulders that blocked out the chilled wind. Kat and Hades each had a small nylon tent. They set them up side by side and close to the fire Hades had constructed out of twigs and moss. The smoke stank, but the flames would serve their purpose. The night would get cold, and predators would soon be in search of a hearty meal.

Kat, Hades, and the others ate dried fruit and meat in silence around the fire. Darquiel seemed to have perked up since the sun went down. She no longer appeared sickly. She was still pale, translucent almost. *Glowing* would be an exaggeration, but it was close to the truth. Close enough to be unnerving.

Kat watched her. The girl made her nervous. She was unpredictable with her changes in physical condition, and that made Kat apprehensive and on edge. The attraction Damian seemed to have for Darquiel also bothered her. It seemed unnatural. During the time they'd been together, Damian had had other lovers, as had she. The women he usually went for were full-bodied and empty-headed. This girl was neither. It was possible that he liked her because she was everything Kat was not: pale, delicate, submissive. Maybe their time together had finally ended. Kat was a firm believer that nothing lasted forever.

After this job, Kat was certain of one thing. Their relationship would never be the same.

Glancing up, Darquiel caught Kat's stare and held it. "Something the matter?"

"You seem different."

"How so?"

"Bolder, more alive."

"The sun makes me . . ." Darquiel paused, as if searching for the right word, " . . . sick. At night I feel much more myself, whole."

Kat tossed a stick into the fire, sending sparks into the air. "It's more than that. You're even different from when we saw you in the bar."

Darquiel smiled. "Must be the outdoors. Nature obviously agrees with me."

"Yes, obviously." Kat stood. "Time for sleep. We'll need to be up and gone by sunrise. It's still another day's ride until we reach the wastelands. I'll be first watch." Picking up her shotgun, she cradled it against her side. She felt more secure with it in her hands.

Hades pushed to his feet. "Sounds good to me. Wake me in a few hours to relieve you." He unzipped his tent and crawled in. "Sure you don't want to join me and let them keep watch?"

Kat shook her head. "Tempting but not likely."

He winked and then did up the flap.

Damian glanced to the other tent and then back to Kat. He studied her for a moment and then looked away, turning to Darquiel. "I guess we'll share the other one."

They both stood and moved to the nylon structure. Damian

unzipped it and Darquiel crawled in. Before he slid through, he regarded Kat. "G'night."

"Sure," she responded, avoiding his gaze.

"Kat, I . . ."

She put up her hand to stop his next words. She didn't want to hear any apologies. Regrets only made things more complicated. From day one, she had told him he was free to be with whomever he wanted. That they were not a married couple and never would be. Still, to see him with this particular woman twisted Kat's insides.

Without another word, Damian went through the opening, zipping it up behind him.

Kat tossed some more sticks onto the waning fire and settled down beside it. She didn't want to be too comfortable or she might doze off. The predators in the surrounding trees weren't the only things that worried her.

She had a dreadful feeling that their guide, Darquiel, was hiding something. Something that could prove to be more dangerous than any starving, vicious four-legged beast.

Hades startled awake. Sitting up, he strained to listen. Had something outside woken him, or was it the dreams again? He rubbed a hand over his face to scrub away the residuals of the images he had been fighting with for the past few nights. Nightmares. The same ones he'd been having since the night before meeting up with Kat in the bar.

He replayed the twisted images of his sleeping mind. A dark, damp room, lots of blood, and an exquisite naked woman hanging in chains from the lofty ceiling. Every time he could only see her back, but whoever it was, she had the nicest, roundest ass he'd ever seen. The dream must have been triggered by having Kat's leather-clad backside against his groin.

He hoped the dreams weren't like the others he'd had through his life. His mother used to call him a Dream Seer because of the premonitions he'd had as a boy. Hades didn't believe in spooks and ghouls and witchcraft, but he couldn't deny that as a boy he'd had many dreams of things that did come true. The events didn't always happen exactly as he imagined, but were close enough that he would sometimes fear going to sleep.

The last one he'd had was in his thirteenth year, when he had dreamed of his mother. Two months later, she died, just as he'd predicted. Ever since then, having agonized over the pain of his mother's death, Hades had subconsciously chosen not to believe in his premonitions.

He rubbed his eyes again. As long as he was awake, he might as well relieve Kat.

He crawled out onto the ground and studied the fire, noting the low flickering flame in desperate need of attention. Eyes wide and alert, Kat sat cross-legged beside it, staring off into the darkness. Moving toward her, he noted the glossy look in her dark green eyes. A trance, possibly? She hadn't made any notice of his presence.

"Kat?" He snapped his fingers in front of her. She didn't flinch. "Kat!" he repeated close to her ear. Still no response.

He hunkered down in front of her and searched her face. She stared straight ahead, right through him. Touching her neck, he found her pulse, relieved to discover it strong. Certain drugs could send a person into la-la land. But this seemed different. It was if she were in a state of suspended animation. He had not heard of anything that could do that.

"This is going to sting, babe."

Hades slapped her hard across the face. As she fell over onto her side, her eyes closed and she went limp. Unsure of what to do, Hades stood over her and frowned. Did he hurt her? He hadn't hit her that hard. She had taken worse, he was sure.

Bending over, he touched her on the shoulder and shook her. "Kat?"

Her eyes flashed open and she grabbed his hand. While she

sat up, she twisted his wrist into an impossible position. Cringing from the pain, Hades dropped to his knees.

"Kat, it's me, Hades."

She looked at him, eyes focusing, and then she narrowed them and wriggled her jaw back and forth. "You hit me."

"I had to. You were in some sort of trance."

"What time is it?"

"At least three hours have gone by since you've been on watch."

Abruptly Kat let go of his wrist. "Are you sure?"

He examined the clear night sky and nodded. "Pretty sure."

Jumping to her feet, Kat rushed over to Damian's tent. She unzipped the flap and stuck her head in to find it empty.

"They're gone."

Hades peered into the opening. "Maybe they went for a walk. For privacy."

"Possibly. But someone put a hex on me, and I don't think it was Damian."

She picked up her shotgun and slung it over her shoulder. Before she could march into the outlining trees, Hades grabbed her arm, pulling her back.

"You're going to get someone killed."

She yanked her arm away. "Yes, that's the whole idea."

"What if Damian gets in the way? Do you want to kill him, too?"

Kat stared up at him, her brow furrowed.

"Well?" Hades prompted.

"I'm thinking."

"Damnit, Kat. I'm going in first. You follow behind. I will assess the situation and determine the best course of action."

"Like hell you will." She pushed past him.

He grabbed her by the hair and yanked her back. She yelped indignantly. "You will do as I say, or you will wish you never met me."

"I already do."

Pulling her head closer, he stared into her upturned face. Her full, parted lips begged him to kiss her. She was the sexiest and most aggravating woman he had ever met.

"Liar." He pushed her away.

Kat rubbed her head and frowned. "You didn't have to pull so hard."

Before he entered the trees, Hades turned and grinned. "Yes, I did."

They crept through the trees, listening for any sign of Damian and Darquiel. Kat was unsure which way they went, but the woods were not that large; she and Hades would easily be able to cover every inch of it before sunrise. If Damian and Darquiel were in there, they'd find them.

As Hades scanned the surrounding area, Kat watched him. She resented his earlier assessment but had to agree. She was angry and would let her emotions dictate the outcome of any altercation. If Damian got in the way of her attack on Darquiel, she might not kill him, but she would surely injure him.

Betrayal pricked her heart. He had allowed his new pet to do something to her. Not once in the last three years of their relationship had Damian allowed any harm to come to her if he could prevent it. One time a year ago he had been offered a disgusting amount of money to deceive her, and he had refused. Treachery over money, she could almost understand, but this, over this woman, she could not and would not comprehend.

Almost at the edge of the woods, Hades stopped and kneeled down. Kat followed his lead and crawled up to his position. He touched his eyes and pointed to the small clearing. Kat squinted into the dark. The full moon illuminated the area and she could clearly see two figures lying in the grassy meadow. Damian was on his back, his pants pushed to his ankles. Darquiel knelt over him, his erect cock in her long, slim hand.

"You see, I was right," Hades whispered.

Kat didn't answer but kept watch on the couple. Darquiel bent forward and put her lips to his cock, kissing it. Kat could hear Damian moan. Darquiel opened her mouth and slid him in, moving up and down in quick strokes.

Hades turned to her and winked. "Give you any ideas?"

Fuck you, she mouthed.

"That's the idea."

Kat punched him in the arm. It had no effect. It was like punching a wall. Her hand stung, but wasn't about to let him know. Her dignity stood in the way.

Hades leaned in close to her, his eyes glinting in the moonlight. "Let's leave them and go back and have our own fun."

This close, she could smell him. Sweat, leather, and male. A delicious combination. She cringed and tried to pull away, but landed on her ass. He moved closer and touched her leg. Even through the leather of her pants, she could feel his heat. If she didn't move soon, she'd be in trouble.

The moans that drifted across the clearing didn't help in squashing her libido. In fact, the erotic sounds revved it up. She felt her insides tighten and her sex dampen. She could not deny her attraction to Hades. He was just the type of guy she liked. Big, strong, and mean. But there was just one problem—he would not be her toy. In fact, they would struggle in the bed for supremacy. She was not quite sure if she wanted to win. And that fact kept her from taking him right there, right now.

"Don't." She scooted away from him.

"I can smell you, Kat. I know you want me." He cupped her cheek and rubbed a thumb over her quivering lips. "And I want you, too, more than anything I've ever wanted in my life."

Kat took in a deep breath as Hades leaned forward. They were inches apart. She could feel his hot breath on her face. She didn't pull back when he pressed his lips to hers. Kat's restraint broke and she accepted what he offered.

Grabbing his jacket, she pulled him closer. Savagely they kissed, nipping playfully at each other's lips. She groaned low in her throat as he moved his hand down to her breast, squeezing her through the fabric of her shirt.

A cry rang out in the night.

Kat pushed Hades away and turned toward the clearing.

"What was that?" Hades asked.

"Damian."

Kneeling between Damian's legs, Darquiel nestled into his groin. Clearly in pain, Damian bowed his back and shook his head from side to side. But his cock, still hard and standing straight, indicated intense pleasure as well.

"What is she doing?" Hades queried.

Kat shook her head and continued to watch. Damian began to scream. In two seconds flat Kat pushed to her feet and ran across the field. Slinging the shotgun forward, she pumped a round into the chamber.

As Kat neared their forms, Darquiel raised her head. Blood glistened on her lips and chin in the pale moonlight. Her eyes widened as she saw Kat barreling toward her with the weapon aimed. Jumping to her feet, Darquiel held out her hands in defense. Kat ran right into her, ramming the other woman's gut.

They fell to the ground, Kat on top, the gun jammed between them. Kat glared down at Darquiel, rage making her see red, her finger twitching on the trigger.

Sneering, Darquiel pushed with her arms. Kat lifted in the air and flew backward, landing hard on her ass about seven feet away.

Kat shook her head and got to her feet. The impact had knocked the breath from her lungs. It felt like she had fallen out of a two-story window. Lifting her head, she stared at Darquiel. The girl was freakishly strong.

Damian was now up and kneeling at Darquiel's feet, his

arms wrapped around her legs, cowering next to her, protecting her with his body.

Kat raised the gun. "Move, Damian."

He shook his head, but refused to look at Kat.

Hades took a step toward Kat. "Don't kill her."

"She was going to kill him."

Hades glanced at Darquiel, his brow crinkled in thought. "No, I don't think so."

"She was feeding from me," Damian sputtered. "She needs blood to sustain her life."

"*Move, Damian!*" Kat's hands shook with rage. She'd never been this fueled by anger before. Most times she handled situations with calm, cool precision. But not this time. This time it was way too personal.

Damian stood and shielded Darquiel with his own body, his pants still bunched at his ankles. Blood dripped down his leg from two small holes in his upper thigh.

"She's inhuman, Damian. She's trapped you."

Darquiel stepped from behind Damian, placing a pale hand on his shoulder, seeming to comfort. "I am a vampyre. I am allergic to the sun, and I need blood to live. Without it I would eventually starve to death no matter how much food I ate."

Kat stared at her, the gun steady and sure in her hands. She just needed one clean shot, but Damian was too close. He would jump in front of the bullet, she was sure.

"What did you do to my head?" Kat demanded.

"I clouded it. An easy trick to learn."

Damian pleaded, reaching out to Kat. "Put down the gun. I can explain this."

"Maybe if you pulled up your pants, she'd listen," Hades said while his hand fell to the knife sheath strapped to his thigh.

Struggling to pull up his pants, Damian winced as the fabric brushed over his bite marks. When he had his pants fastened, he started toward Kat.

"Stay where you are," Kat advised, her voice calm despite the quivers racing through her body.

Damian flinched at her cold voice but stilled in midstride. "Why? You have nothing to fear from me."

"But I do from her? Is that what you're saying?" Kat prompted.

"No. That's not what I meant. Kat, you don't understand. If I, if we could explain, you would see that this . . . that this was nothing."

"I'm listening. And it better be good or I'll blow her fucking head off."

"Could we go back to camp and sit down and talk?" Damian suggested.

"No," Kat commanded. "We do this here, now. I will not give her a chance to overpower me."

Damian stumbled sideways. "Well, I'm sitting. I feel a little faint." He dropped to the ground, landing smartly on his ass.

Darquiel rushed to him, concern furrowing her brow.

"You might as well sit with him," Kat growled, gesturing with her weapon.

Darquiel sat cross-legged beside Damian, putting her arm around him as he leaned into her. Kat found the act more possessive than comforting.

Kat nodded to her. "Talk."

"When I was a girl of fifteen, I traveled to the Vanquished City with my mom and dad and little brother. My dad was a real archaeologist. He located and excavated lost technology to enable us to progress as a society. To study what went wrong the first time around." Her voice was cold and calm as she spoke. "We made camp at the perimeter of the city. That first night, we were attacked. Our guide was the first to be slaughtered. His heart was ripped from his body. They put it in a plastic bag and took it with them. I know," she paused, "because I held it in my hands later that night."

Kat could only imagine the girl's horror at what she had experienced. Just hearing about it made Kat's skin crawl.

"My mom and dad were next. They had their throats torn out and their bodily fluids were consumed. My dear little brother was the last to die. He had hidden at the first sign of violence. But they soon found him. They could smell his fear." She shivered slightly and Damian placed his hand on her leg. "They made me watch as the leader, Baruch, slit his throat with a small razor he had imbedded in his thumb. He did it slowly, and I watched as every spasm of pain flashed across Tom's face. They took me with them to their lair beneath the city. Baruch took a liking to me. He thought my pain looked exquisite etched across my pale, innocent face." She hugged Damian closer to her, but kept Kat's gaze. "You see, I know what hell looks like. It's the face of my brother as he slowly died from blood loss, pain and suffering swimming in his clear blue eyes. You can point whatever you like at me, but I have already died and been to hell. There is nothing you can do to me that would be worse."

Kat continued to watch Darquiel, the gun still raised. She had heard stories about cannibals living in the wastelands, blood rituals, and human sacrifices. She hadn't believed them. She couldn't believe that humans could do that to each other. But, obviously, they could do a lot worse.

She felt sorrow for Darquiel's plight, but still didn't trust her. Darquiel had been made into something unnatural and tainted. Could her mind have sustained such torture and torment without becoming twisted and corrupted? That was the question Kat was not sure she could risk finding the answer to. It might kill them all.

"If your story is true, then how could we possibly trust you? You could be leading us into a trap. An ambush for your bloodsucking friends."

Damian jumped to his feet and charged toward her. "You bitch! How can you say such a thing?"

Hades grabbed him before he could reach Kat and the shotgun she still held steady and firm. "Don't be stupid. If the blood wasn't pumping elsewhere in your body, you would realize she has a sound point," Hades said.

"Damian, I'd put you down if I knew you weren't under her influence," Kat hissed between clenched teeth. Damian slumped against Hades.

Darquiel stood. "Damian, it's okay. Her question is valid." She turned toward Kat. "You have no reason to trust me, and there is no guarantee I can give you that you will accept. So it seems we are at an impasse."

Kat turned her gaze to Damian. His face was drawn and tired. He met her stare, his eyes pleading, begging her. She ignored them.

Her attention returned to Darquiel. "As soon as we reach the city's border, you will leave. If you don't, I will blow you away. We'll be picking off your remains for days."

Darquiel nodded. "Agreed."

"No!" Damian shrieked.

Kat ignored his plea. "The rest of the time you will be bound. I will not take any chances."

Darquiel nodded again.

Kat lowered her gun and glanced up into the sky. "Let's break camp and get on our way. It will be dawn soon."

When Hades let go of Damian, he rushed to Darquiel and hugged her hard.

"You two, go first." She motioned with her weapon toward the woods.

Darquiel and Damian trudged forward. Kat followed with Hades close behind. They returned to camp without incident and started to pack up to get back on the road. The wastelands were only a day away, and who knew what was waiting for them there.

Eyeing Damian and Darquiel, Kat rolled up her tent and shoved it into the canvas bag. Damian was reluctantly putting away their food and water supplies while watching Darquiel slumped against a tree, her wrists tied tight. Kat could feel her well-laid plans unraveling thread by thread.

She had not counted on trouble from their guide, or the fact that Darquiel enthralled Damian to the point where Kat felt him slipping away from her—something she thought would never happen. She wasn't overly conceited to think that he would never find someone else, but she hadn't expected it this way or with this girl. After the hunt, Kat assumed that she and Damian would be partying it up somewhere with the money they got from the treasure. It was obvious now that that wasn't going to happen.

As she strapped bags to her bike, Kat's gaze swayed to Hades. He, too, fastened gear onto his saddlebags. Hades was another unexpected problem, and the last person she thought she'd ever team up with. For more years than she could remember, the two of them had been battling, unseen and apart, for treasure hunts. His presence, although invisible, continually pressed down on her. Always she felt like she had to compete with him, outdo him, and impress him. Now that she'd ended up here, face-to-face with him, she felt other, unwelcome emotions.

She was starting to like him.

Certainly, he pulled at her carnally. The man possessed a sexy, dark, and dangerous aura that made her mouth water and her lower parts boil. But there were other qualities about him that were starting to eat at her insides. He was charming in a wolfish way, which of course turned her on even more and made her laugh. Life didn't bring her much to laugh about. So she found his easygoing manner refreshing.

With Damian slowly pulling away, Hades's presence felt welcoming. It was just that Kat had no idea what to do with the sensation and with the feelings creeping up on her. Emotions didn't work for her. They hadn't helped her in the past, and she couldn't imagine what good they would be in the future. They would get in her way, especially on the most dangerous hunt of her life.

While she shoved another pack into her saddlebag, she did the same with her emotions. Pushing them deep inside where she hoped the feelings would stay. The last thing she needed was to get involved with Hades. He was trouble in more ways than she wanted to consider.

7

After another grueling twelve hours on the road, the group pulled over into a boggy clearing surrounded by a clump of bushes and several huge boulders. It wasn't the most pleasant spot to camp, with its soft ground and putrid smell, but at least it had water. Not clean clear water, but enough to wash in and siphon off for drinking.

Kat unpacked her tent and pitched it near the boulders to block out the increasing wind and to protect her back. Hades, Damian, and Darquiel did their own housekeeping and then settled down to eat. Since they were occupied, Kat thought it would be an opportune time for her to change clothes and wash. Taking her pack, she ducked behind the scragily bushes.

Stripping off her sodden and dirty T-shirt, Kat crouched down next to the swamp and dipped the fabric into the water. Her skin felt gritty and grimy after the long ride. Even with her jacket on, dirt had managed to coat her skin. She stood and rubbed her wet T-shirt over her torso and under her arms. What she wouldn't give for a bath right about now. A nice, long, hot bath with scented soap.

Closing her eyes, she indulged in her fantasy, and continued to trail the wet cloth over her skin, circling her breasts and down to her navel. If she'd been more secluded, Kat might have considered taking off her pants and completing the job.

"How's the water?"

As Kat's eyes sprang open, she brought up the T-shirt to her breasts. But by the look in Hades's eyes, he'd been watching her. Covering herself now didn't make a difference. He'd already seen the goods.

Turning, she gave him her back and continued to wash her arms and shoulders. She wouldn't give Hades the satisfaction of seeing her blush. She was surprised to find that she almost had.

"It's wet," she commented, trying to sound casual, as if his presence didn't affect her. In reality her heart had picked up a few beats and shivers of anticipation tingled over her flesh. When he stepped up behind her, close enough to touch, Kat had to stop herself from spinning around and embracing him.

"Want me to wash you?"

She could hear the sexual proposition in his question. And she was more than tempted to take it. More than she wanted to admit.

"I got it, thanks," she said as she rubbed the cloth up her neck.

Suddenly cool liquid dribbled down her back, bringing instant relief to the sweltering heat. A low moan escaped her lips before she could stop it. She glanced over her shoulder as Hades, his sexy dimple winking at her, wrung out his bandanna above her again.

"How's that feel?"

She smiled, reluctantly charmed by the rogue. "Fantastic."

"Good, because you're doing me later."

Kat burst out laughing, unable to stop herself. The man had magnetism; that was for sure. She found it impossible to dislike him.

"Do women really fall for your wit and charm?"

"No. It's my body they can't resist." He flexed his brawny arm. His bicep bulged like a rock under his skin. Impressive. But Kat's gaze traveled lower. She imagined he had interesting bulges all over his powerful frame.

He smiled when he noticed her wandering eyes, and took a step closer to her. Kat turned her head around and braced herself for what she knew was coming.

He touched her shoulder first, caressing her skin with the gentle stroke of his thumb. She sucked in a breath as he moved his hands down her back, rubbing her tight, sore muscles in little circles.

Another groan escaped her lips.

Hades chuckled. "Enjoying this?"

"Hell, yeah. I can't remember the last time I had a good back massage," Kat confessed.

Positioning his palms near her shoulders, he started to massage, pushing his thumbs under her hair along the back of her neck. "Damian's neglecting his duties?"

Although his words were said casually, Kat could hear the tension in his timbre. Was he jealous? He had no claim on her. His jealousy was misplaced. Damian and she had an open relationship. If Kat wanted to pursue something more with Hades, she would.

"None of your business," Kat said as she rotated her neck, enjoying his strong hands on her flesh. She wanted to fall into him and let his hands roam lower in more needy places.

"Hmm, what if I want to make it my business?" He nuzzled his face into her hair and started to slide his hands down over her chest.

She let out a low moan as his large, meaty palms covered her breasts possessively as if he had every right to them. While he squeezed and molded, rubbing his thumbs over her tight peaks,

Kat thought he could have her fleshy mounds, just as long as he didn't stop the delicious things he was doing to them.

Pushing aside her hair with his nose, Hades pressed his lips to the side of her throat. "I love the smell of your skin." He trailed his tongue up and down her neck, stopping to suck on a particularly sensitive spot just below her ear.

With a sigh, Kat leaned into him. He felt so good. Strong and sturdy. Damian had never felt that way, though he was certainly strong; he could lift her off the ground and fuck her against a wall, even had on several occasions. He could hold his own in a fight, but he had always seemed frail to her, as though one mighty blow of a powerful wind would knock him over like a domino.

In comparison, Hades was like a rock. There was no doubt in Kat's mind that he could face anything and remain standing, stable and unaffected. She recognized herself in him. And that was a frightening realization.

Kat closed her eyes as he continued to squeeze her breasts, pinching and pulling her nipples into hard, tight peaks. Then she felt one hand move down her body to her stomach. He flattened his hand on her belly and pulled her tight against him. There was no mistaking the iron length of him digging into her ass.

"Can you feel how hard I am for you, Kat?

"Yes," she said sighing. She wanted him; there was no doubt about it. Her legs trembled at the thought of him buried in between them. Deep into her throbbing pussy.

Hades continued to move his hand down. With a flick of his thumb and finger, he undid the button on her leather pants. He inched past the waistband and into the soft curls on her mound. With a moan he slid them farther and parted her plump nether lips.

Her body burned for him, but it was still her mind that

fought the urges. Nothing but problems would come from their union. Kat didn't need any more hitches in her life.

Opening her eyes, she moved her head, pulling away from his mouth, which was still nibbling on her neck. "Hades, I—"

"Shut up, Kat, and let your body speak. I know you want me just as much as I want you." He slid his fingers back and forth in her cleft. "I can feel your lust on my fingers."

As Kat grabbed his hand at her crotch and pulled it out of her pants, she pushed away and turned to face him. Anger flared through her. "Shut up? What do you mean, shut up? Where do you come off telling me to shut up?"

Hades chuckled and rubbed a hand over his swollen crotch. "Woman, you're killing me, here."

She took a step forward and got in his face. "You're lucky I don't kill you, asshole."

Hades smiled and chucked her under the chin. "I love it when you talk dirty."

Clenching her hand into a tight fist, Kat pulled back her arm to punch Hades in the mouth. Before she could swing, Damian's voice rang through the air.

"Kat! We got company!"

Both Kat and Hades sprang into action. While Kat did up her pants, Hades tossed her a dry T-shirt from her pack.

He winked at her as he unsheathed his knives from his leg straps. "To be continued."

"In your dreams." Kat slid out two of her knives, also strapped to her thighs. She twirled them once into attack position and then followed Hades to their camp. She swore to herself, knowing that her shotgun was sitting on the ground near her tent. It was no good to her there.

Before she could push through the bushes, Hades grabbed her arm and pulled her down to the ground.

"What are you doing?" She tried to pull from his grip.

"Take a look." He nodded toward a small break in the foliage.

Peering through the bushes, Kat immediately saw two problems. One, Damian and Darquiel were being held at gunpoint by a big, ugly hunter in an ash-gray cloak, and two, there were two more just like him waiting for her and Hades to come out of the trees.

"Damnit," Kat swore under her breath. "Where did those scumbags get guns?"

"Don't know. Stole them, is my guess. I'm more worried about how much ammo they have. We have to think before we go running in there or we'll all end up dead."

"Yeah, everyone but Darquiel."

Kat scanned Darquiel through the leaves again. Even from this distance she could see the rage swimming in her pale face. Kat wondered what it would take for the girl to unleash the freakish strength she had growing inside her.

"What are you thinking?"

"I'm thinking we need to unchain our little weapon of mass destruction," Kat mused.

"How do you know she'll do what you think she'll do?"

"Basic laws of survival." Kat smiled as she pushed through the bushes a little giving, herself a good view of Darquiel but still hidden from their attackers. "Kill or be killed."

One of the hunters stepped forward in the general vicinity of where Kat and Hades hid. "You have two minutes to come out or we'll kill them both."

Kat pushed back the violent urge to rush out and fight. She supposed if Hades hadn't stopped her at the bushes, she would have. And, most probably, would have ended up with a few bullets in her, dead before she could reach the assailants. Not only did the man inflame her body, he also made her stop and think. Something her hotheaded impetuousness often kept her from doing on a daily basis. Damn him, if he wasn't turning out to be a good partner.

She had a plan. She just hoped it worked. If not, they would die. Well, she summarized, they had to go sometime. Why not now?

"Go ahead, kill them. I've grown tired of the boy, and the girl, well, I just don't like her."

She could see Damian bristle at her comments. But Darquiel looked calm as she sat on the ground next to the gunman. She wondered if the girl knew what she was planning.

The hunter licked his lips nervously. "I should have known you'd sacrifice these two for your own skin, Hell Kat. You're not known for your generosity."

"That's right. You best remember that. Because when you beg me for mercy, you know I won't give you any."

Hades leaned into the bushes close to her and whispered, "What are you doing?"

"When I say, 'Now,' rush in, knives in the air."

Patting her on the shoulder, he nodded. "I'll trust you. But next time I get to decide how we're going to die, okay?"

Kat grinned. "Deal."

With a soft chuckle Hades pulled away and positioned himself a few feet from her, ready to go when she said the word. She hoped they got out of this one alive and unscathed. Because if they did, she just might let Hades back into her pants.

Under her breath, she counted to three. On three, she stood and flung one of her knives toward the gunman covering Damian and Darquiel. The knife missed the mark and landed in the ground, directly in front of Darquiel. She ducked back down into the bushes.

Perfect shot.

The gunman laughed. "You missed, bitch."

Darquiel leaned forward and put her bound hands around the knife. "No, she didn't."

With one swipe up, the ropes were sliced through on the blade, and Darquiel was loose.

Before the gunman could swing the barrel down, Darquiel was on him, tearing through his leg with her nails and teeth. He screamed as she ripped open his flesh.

Kat wanted to turn away from the grisly scene, but it was the perfect distraction. The other two hunters turned and swung their guns toward the battle.

"Now!"

Kat leaped out of the bushes and started running. In her peripheral she saw Hades matching her stride for stride. He pulled back his arm and threw one of his knives and then the other. One blade took one of the hunters in the side, and the second knife struck his thigh. As the hunter turned in reaction to the attack, Kat threw her blade and he caught it in the neck. As he went down, he turned his shotgun toward her and pulled the trigger.

The sound was deafening, like the explosive crack of thunder.

As the clatter roared in her head and the bullet sped toward her, two things raced through Kat's mind. *If I jump, can I reach my shotgun, and what if I never get another chance to kiss Hades?* Before she could ponder either one of these things too seriously, she was knocked to the ground by a large mass of black leather.

The bullet slammed into the ground one foot from where she had been running.

With a grunt, Hades rolled off her, reached for her weapon, and sprang to his feet. He pumped one round into the hunter still standing trying to load his own chamber.

Kat scrambled to her feet as the final hunter dropped to the ground, the hole in his chest still smoking. Hades turned and winked at her, handing back her shotgun.

She nodded to him with appreciation that he didn't make a

big deal out of saving her life. For only knowing her a few days, the man knew when to push and when not to. It amazed her how in sync they seemed.

She shook off the creeping emotions and turned toward Damian. He stood transfixed, staring at Darquiel kneeling on the ground. Kat went to him and nudged him in the shoulder. "Are you all right?"

He didn't answer, nor did he indicate he had heard her. Kat examined the spot where he stared. The scene made her gorge rise, but she swallowed down the urge to vomit.

Darquiel was covered in blood. And the dead hunter had been ripped open. She was crouched a foot away from the ravaged body, licking the remaining blood off her fingers.

Turning her head, Darquiel glanced up at Kat and smiled. Kat didn't like the savage stare in her black eyes.

"Clean up. We need to move the bodies. We don't want predators showing up searching for a meal." As Kat said this, she knew she was already looking at one. And this predator was extremely intelligent. More so than she let on.

Turning, Kat glanced at Damian. He still stared, wide-eyed, at Darquiel. Kat nudged him again. This time he looked up at her, his eyes glossy and frightened.

"Get a good look, Damian. You can't turn back now. This is what you chose. Her. Deal with it."

Leaving him to deal with his decisions, Kat marched over to where the other bodies lay. She'd check to see if they were still alive and then they needed to dispose of them somewhere away from their camp. Full darkness had set in. Dawn would come before long and they still had a long journey ahead of them.

The Vanquished City was calling, and nothing was going to stop her, not even death itself.

8

After another long ride Kat stopped her bike right at the end of the road. It seemed as though the concrete had been cut off with a large, jagged hatchet. Spread out before her in a desolate sweep of rusty dirt and rock, she saw a place devoid of all life. No trees grew there, not even grass. No small trickle of water carved a path through the ground. A long stretch of ravaged land, the wastelands, divided the Vanquished City from the rest of the plains. It started abruptly, as if some invisible barrier separated it from the trees and grass out of which they had just driven.

Kat had never seen such a barren desert before. The outer rims were desolate and empty, but one could still see remnants of humanity in the crumbled concrete and neglected, burned-out, dilapidated buildings. But here, there was nothing. Just a straight stretch of reddish earth and rock. A few hills of jagged stone stood out obscenely from the scorched ground here and there, but she could still see for miles in either direction.

She turned to look at Hades, finding a mirror image of her shock and awe evident on his face.

"I have heard of it, but I never thought this was possible."

"Me neither." She gaped around again, shaking her head in disbelief. "It's . . ."

"Scary as hell," Damian murmured from behind her on the bike.

Kat nodded. Squinting toward the horizon, she could almost make out a few peaks. She hoped they were the remnants of Vanquished City.

"How far do you think this stretches?" she asked Hades.

He shook his head. "Don't know. From the looks of it, a while."

She glanced at Darquiel. "Do you know?"

"It's not more than four hours to the city's boundaries."

"Are you sure?"

"No. I haven't been this way before. But I *feel* like it's not far." Darquiel shivered.

Kat grabbed her canteen and took a swig of water. She wiped the sweat that already beaded on her top lip. "We have about three hours to full noon. If we're caught out on these plains, we'll fry."

"The bikes won't last either. They'll overheat for sure," Hades stated.

"We could wait till dark," Darquiel suggested.

Kat looked back at her and smirked. "And wait until God knows what comes out to play? No, thank you. I want to see what I'm shooting."

"If we have a straight stretch, we can make it," Hades declared.

Kat regarded Hades and nodded in agreement. "Let's do it."

"Let's fill up the bikes first. Don't want to run out of gas." Hades booted out the kickstand and turned off the bike. Kat did the same. He unstrapped the gas cans from the back, uncapped his fuel tank, and filled up. Then he did the same on

Kat's bike until the gas can was almost empty. A small amount swished around at the bottom.

"Will we be able to find more gas?" Damian asked, worry furrowing his brow.

Hades shrugged. "Don't know. Should be able to, but it's not certain."

"Then what do we do?"

"Walk." Hades straddled the bike again and kicked it over. It roared to life. Watching Kat, he grinned. "Race you."

Kat returned the smile. She couldn't help it. The man found a good time in everything he did. "You're on." She revved the bike. Damian knowingly clutched her around her hips. This wasn't the first time they had raced with reckless abandon.

Behind Hades, Darquiel squeezed her eyes shut and wrapped her arms around his waist, clutching her hands together to turn her knuckles white.

Kat and Hades both turned their clutches and the bikes jerked forward and jumped off the edge of the road onto the hardened dirt. Creating long, dusty tails, they raced straight toward the horizon, spraying up dirt in their wake.

An hour gone, Kat's hair and body were soaked with sweat. The wind from the racing gave little relief. She could feel Damian's sweaty hands on her waist even through the leather. He, too, must be suffering. The wind did not hit him square on.

The leather she wore was stifling, but she wore it for other purposes. It protected her from things other than heat. The leather stopped the UV rays from scorching holes in her skin. She may sweat to death, but she wouldn't burn. And if she ever took a spill on the bike, the tough material would protect her from road rash.

After racing for a half hour, they both had brought their speed down a little. A silent concession had been made. Neither would win this race, so they slowed to a comfortable speed.

"Take the right handle," she said to Damian.

He snuggled closer into her and did as instructed. They had performed this maneuver many times before. Kat had no fear of falling.

Kat held the canteen she had hanging around her neck and took a big swallow and then another. The third she slowly let trickle down her chin and down her neck. The water and wind gave some reprieve from the heat.

As she slung the canteen over her shoulder to Damian, Kat took back the handle while he drank. She glanced over at Hades and noticed he also sipped from his flask, but had no need for another hand on his handle. After one last long swig, he swung it over his shoulder to Darquiel. Pressed tightly against his back, eyes squeezed shut, she would not relinquish her hold for a drink.

Kat shook her head. She shouldn't care. The girl was as good as dead in her mind. Before long the sun would fry her. It was rising quickly in the brilliant blue of the sky. It would not be long before it was at its zenith and its deathly rays would bake them all into pieces of crispy bacon.

Inching the bike closer to Hades, Kat yelled over the roar of the engines. "What do you think?"

"Doesn't feel like we're even moving. All I can see in every direction is desert."

Kat nodded. She had noticed that, too, but she did think that the peaks on the horizon were getting larger.

"What about those?" She gestured to the dark shapes taking form in the distance.

"Could be rocks."

"Could be scrapers."

"Let's hope they are." Hades smiled and then turned his head. His grin suddenly faded as he reached out with his hand and grabbed her handlebar. "*Stop!*"

Kat turned her hand down on the grip to initiate the brakes.

The tires spun on the loose dirt and gravel. She stomped down on the emergency brake on the foot pedals. She turned the bike and skidded onto the side, sliding across the sand. The bike came to a stop right on the edge of a deep chasm; the rear wheel hung over the edge, sending rocks and gravel tumbling down the ravine.

Swearing, Kat eyed Hades. He had also brought his bike down on the side to stop, but he was not as dangerously close to the edge as she was.

He pushed himself out from under the machine and had to pull Darquiel out. She was weak and looked very near to fainting.

He rushed over to where they were teetering, cowed under the weight of the steel.

"Damian, can you move without pushing on the bike?"

"I think so." Damian relinquished his hold on Kat and scooted up. The bike moved forward. As she felt the weight of the machine begin to reel it over the edge, Kat squeezed her eyes shut. She held on to the handles tightly and tried to stop its motion, but she feared she was not strong enough.

As Damian scooted out, Hades grabbed onto Kat and pulled back. He tugged with all his strength. Kat opened her eyes as she and the motorcycle, which she held deftly in her hands and between her legs, moved back with her. When she could safely scramble out from the tempered and twisted metal without it falling over the edge and taking her with it, she breathed a deep sigh of relief.

She fell backward onto the ground. "That was close."

Hades looked down at her, a troubled expression on his face. He touched her gently on the cheek. "Too close."

The gentle touch on her face disconcerted Kat. Her smile faded as she gazed up into the blue of his eyes. Something flashed there, but it was not lust or anger. A mixture between the two. She felt her stomach flip over.

As quickly as he had touched her, he withdrew his hand. Hades stood and studied the ravine they had nearly driven right into.

Kat scrambled to her feet and brushed at her clothes. Dirt was the least of her worries as she soon felt a throb and sharp pain in her right leg. She peeked down and noticed a tear in her leather pants. Blood leaked through.

"Shit."

Hades turned to her and followed her gaze down to where she fingered the wound. "Is it bad?"

"You know how hard it is to mend leather?"

Hades barked out a full, hearty laugh. Kat grinned back. He stepped next to her and put an arm companionably around her shoulders, pulling her into him. She didn't retreat, but put an arm around his waist in return. They stood like that, gazing across the ravine for a time without words, as if the gaping hole before them said it all.

Breaking the hold, Kat stepped forward to stare into the deep crevice. It appeared that the earth had just cracked open. This was not produced by wind and water, since there was no water for miles. It took thousands of years or a devastating earthquake to produce a canyon like this.

"Can we jump it?" Kat asked.

"Alone maybe. But with two riders on a bike . . . not likely."

Kat looked sideways down the ravine. It stretched for miles. "Do you think there's a bridge?"

"Maybe, but how far is it? We could drive for hours and not find one," Hades replied.

Kat kicked at the dirt. Rocks tumbled over the edge. She glanced behind her at Damian and Darquiel. Darquiel was lying on Damian's cloak, cradled in his lap. He stroked her sweaty brow but met Kat's gaze.

"Ask her if she's seen this ravine before."

Leaning close to Darquiel's ear, Damian spoke to her. He

looked up and shook his head. "There wasn't a ravine when she escaped the city. But she doesn't know how far along this way that she escaped."

Kat peered in both ways down the canyon. "Well, we know this way will eventually take us to the ocean. So the ravine can't go on that way long, or there'd be water rushing at the bottom, and there isn't. And the other way . . ."

"Could go on for miles. More miles than we can risk." Hades glanced at the sky. The sun was moving.

"We could go back," Damian suggested. "Start again at dark."

Kat glanced at Damian's hope-filled face. She shook her head. "No. I won't go back. Let's follow this down toward the ocean. It can't be more than a three-hour drive."

"In three hours we could be crispy critters," Hades pointed out.

"I'd rather ride with smoke trailing off my ass then quit."

Hades nipped her around the waist and pulled her toward him. Bending down, he smashed his mouth to hers. He kissed her thoroughly, urging a small moan from between her lips. He let go just as suddenly and took a distancing step.

"Me, too."

He winked and then turned toward his bike, glancing down at Damian and Darquiel. "Time to get moving."

Kat stood still and watched as Hades took a swig of water from his canteen. He then offered some to Damian, who took it and poured water into Darquiel's thin mouth.

The kiss had stunned her. It had been fierce and smoldering. As his tongue had parted her lips, she could feel the heat between the two of them sizzle in her mouth. She had been kissed a million times before, but never with such determination. Bringing a shaky hand to her mouth, she tried to rub away the feelings the kiss stirred inside—except the feelings had stimulated something deep that no amount of rubbing could erase.

9

For the next two hours they raced alongside the ravine, searching for a bridge or a pass. With the sun near its zenith, lethal rays glared down on them like laser beams. Although Kat had covered up as much as possible, she could still feel the exposed skin on her face redden. The dark goggles protected her eyes, the hood of her cloak protected her head, but her cheeks and lower face were still bare. Her lips were beginning to crack from the extreme heat.

Glancing over at Hades, she spied duplicate red patches on his face. Behind him, Darquiel could barely hang on. She was completely covered, but Kat could plainly see the sweat pour off her. Her cloak was sodden right though. Hades had tied her hands around him for fear that she could not hold on any longer. By the looks of her slumped head, he was right in doing so.

"I can't hold on." Damian's voice was low and hoarse, barely audible over the din of the engine.

Kat swallowed as she heard the defeat in Damian's voice. "Yes, you can. Wrap your hands under my knife strap."

"If I fall I'll pull you off."

"Just do it, damnit!"

She could feel Damian slowly work his hands around the leather strap wrapped around her waist and over her shoulder. He was right. If he fell, he would pull her off. But she would not allow him to give up, not yet. Not when there was still some fight left in her.

Staring ahead, she squinted and willed something to appear in the horizon. They couldn't go on much longer. The sweat that ran off her face stung her eyes. She could feel her throat constrict, feel the flesh inside begin to wither and wrinkle from lack of water. Her canteen was empty. The water that had been left had evaporated in the stifling heat. When she had last popped the cap, steam rose from inside.

"Kat! Look!" Hades pointed to the horizon.

Trying to clear her sight, Kat blinked several times. She could make out a clump of green peaks. They almost appeared to be tall trees. She sighed and glanced at Hades.

He was grinning like a lunatic. "We're going to make it!"

Steam rose from his gas tank. A squeal erupted from within the metal basin. Hades swore and pulled on the brakes. He skidded to an abrupt stop. Dragging Darquiel with him, he got off the bike. He disengaged her hands from his belt and laid her down on the ground. More vapor and smoke erupted from the machine.

Kat had stopped her vehicle ahead of him. Turning it around, she sped back to where he had stopped.

"Fuck!" He kicked the bike. It fell over on its side with a metallic whine. "Fuck!" He kicked in the gas tank. The cap exploded into the air with a distinctive pop. Steam blew out like a whale blasting water out its blowhole.

"What do we do?" Kat asked.

Hades looked at her and then glanced at the rising peaks in the horizon. "Take Damian, drop him off some place safe, and come back and get her." He motioned toward Darquiel, who was lying on her back, her arms out and legs spread. Her chest didn't rise with breath.

"Take her first," Damian croaked.

"Damian, she's done," Kat pointed out.

"Take her." He unhooked his hands from Kat's strap and fell sideways off the bike. Hades caught him and stood him up. His knees wobbled; Hades had to hold him up.

"Fine, put her on," Kat said shaking her head. A fool's errand. The girl was dead.

Hades let Damian slide to the ground. He grabbed Darquiel's arms and dragged her over to Kat's bike. Picking her up, he set her on the back of the bike. She sagged sadly like a rag doll against Kat, so Hades wrapped her arms around Kat's waist and tied her hands together.

"She has no pulse," he whispered to Kat.

"Damian's delusional to think this girl's going to survive. The sun's fried his brains." She glanced at Damian. He was slumped over on his side and watching them intently. "It's his funeral."

Hades packed the rest of the supplies behind Darquiel, squishing her up against Kat. He took a step away and surveyed his handiwork. The motorcycle looked ready to topple over.

"If you make it, I'll be surprised," Hades remarked.

Kat looked at him then. His face was red and sweat soaked his shirt and the bandanna he still had on his bald pate. He grinned. The grin was lopsided as if he no longer had the strength to lift the other side on his upper lip.

"You better hope I do or your head will be a fried egg."

"Hey, I never had much upstairs anyway. It's down below where all my talent lies."

Kat laughed. "If we make it out of this . . . you can show me that talent of yours."

Hades moved up next to the bike, placing his hand on her cheek and rubbing a thumb over her sore lips. "Now that's something to live for." He leaned in close and pressed his mouth softly to hers. "Hurry back."

With awkward movements, Kat turned the machine and revved the engine. She pulled away slowly, careful not to kick back dirt or to topple the bike. Shifting gears, she raced toward the growing peaks.

As the front wheel hit small rocks, she almost lost control but managed to hold on out of desperation more than any skill. She could see the points soar before her. They were green. A beautiful, deep green. The color of newly budded leaves.

She drove for no more than a half hour when she saw a clump of lush trees looming in the distance. The image wavered and she wondered if it was a mirage. She'd heard of these phantom images coming to men and women in dire straits, their brains fried from too much sun. As she grew closer, she could see flourishing green grass beneath the tall trunks. Tilting up her head, she could almost feel a cool breeze on her face and smell salty moisture in the air. If this was a mirage, it was a glorious one, she thought.

The closer she got to the oasis, the greener the colors seemed. She stopped and marveled at the refuge before her. Propping up the bike, she dismounted, grabbing Darquiel's arms as she swung her leg over. She pulled the girl across the dirt and onto the green carpet of grass to lay her down in a circle of shade. Kat brushed her hand over the grass. It felt soft like velvet under her palm. She ripped out a handful and shoved it into her mouth.

Chewing quickly, she sucked on the liquid that erupted from within. The taste was tart but pleasant. Kat thought she had never tasted anything so good. She moved to the bike and unpacked the gear. Grabbing her canteen, she scanned the surroundings. There had to be water nearby. She could smell it in the air.

Kat crouched down at the base of one of the trees, digging at the ground around it. When she pushed down, her hand came away damp. She dug deeper into the dark soil. Soon a little pool of water rose to the surface. As she dipped her canteen into it, dirt and little bits of grass went in with the liquid. It didn't matter. Only the water mattered.

As fast as she could, Kat returned to her bike, removed all the gear, and turned it toward the way she came. Speed was integral. Hades and Damian would not last long out in this heat. Damian, she was certain, was on his last legs.

When she came upon them, Hades had Damian slung over his shoulder, slowly staggering forward. She raced to him, spinning the bike around at the last moment. Hades set Damian down behind her on the seat. Damian was barely able to lift his arms around her.

"Wrap his hands around my holster."

Hades did as she asked.

Opening her canteen, she took a swallow and handed it to Hades. He took it and put it to his lips, taking a small swallow. Dirt and debris stuck to his mouth. He smiled. Green pieces of grass stuck in his teeth.

"You're brilliant."

"You can call me whatever you want after I save us all." She held out her hand. "Give me your canteen."

Hades untangled the cord from around his neck and gave it to her. Stumbling to the right, Hades had to grab the bike for support.

"I'll be back," Kat promised. "Don't die on me."

"Die? Damn, girl, I don't even know what that word means."

Kat managed a smile. The man was relentless. They were the same in so many ways. More than she ever thought possible. Before she revved the bike and sped to the oasis, she glanced at him, hoping it wouldn't be the last time.

The bike sputtered once before they reached the refuge.

Damian was barely hanging on when she stopped on the green. After dismounting, she helped him lie down next to Darquiel. Kat noticed that the girl had not moved while she was gone.

Kat rushed to the tree and dug out more water, filling the canteen. She hunkered down next to Damian and lifted his head. He drank a little and then gulped more as the liquid soothed his parched throat. "Not so much. You'll get sick."

She took back the canteen and filled it again and then got on the bike. She glanced at Damian. He was watching her through the thin slits of his eyes.

"Hades . . ." Damian croaked. "He's a good man."

"So are you, Damian."

"But just not the right man." He smiled briefly and then closed his eyes, rolling over to put an arm across Darquiel.

Kat watched him snuggle close to Darquiel. She sighed and kicked over the bike. There would be time for regrets, but now was not it. She turned the bike and raced back into the wastelands.

She had another man to rescue.

Hades stumbled along the dirt path. The bandanna covering his head was no longer blocking out the sun's rays. He could feel the skin on his scalp redden. Soon it would blacken and begin to crack, like roasted pig too long on the spit. Putting up the hood on his cloak, he slumped forward. To avoid the blazing rays, he would have to watch his feet. He hoped he didn't stumble into the ravine.

This was not the way he thought he'd die. He'd been in so many knife and gunfights that he was certain he would die riddled by bullets or from a gut wound he could not sew up. *Burning to a crisp* and *dehydration from profuse sweating* were not on his list of cool ways to kick the bucket.

He blundered over a small rock and nearly fell. As he put out his hand to steady himself, he started to laugh hysterically.

Irony sucked. He was going to trip over some insignificant piece of gravel and topple head on into the chasm like a bumbling idiot.

Glancing up toward the wavering horizon, he wondered if Kat would make it back to him. Chances were slim to none. But if the girl had any fight left in her, he knew he would see her again. What she lacked in brutal strength she made up for in cunning and determination.

Hades raised his goggles and wiped the sweat from his stinging eyes. He set them snugly in place and then took a sip from his canteen. The dirt and debris had settled on the bottom, so the water was nearly clear. It tasted like ambrosia as he filled his mouth. He had never tasted anything so refreshing, except for maybe Kat.

When he kissed her, he felt like he had just taken a breath of clean, cool air. She tasted like a spring breeze on the cusp of summer. If he got another chance, he wondered if he could turn that brisk taste into something warm and liquid. If he could turn her rigidity into surrender.

He desperately wanted that, wanted her. He'd never met another woman he found to be his equal in every way. Actually, he had never met a woman he would have made much effort for. He'd had his share of sexual liaisons. The prostitutes of various townships knew him well. Those women were good at what they did and carried no complications such as loyalty or friendship—feelings he was starting to harbor for Kat.

Just as strong-willed, disciplined, cunning, and determined as he, Kat was ever his equal. Possibly even more. He easily could have dropped his guard for her, to take her. And although he could feel her want, feel her desire for him, she held back. She kept those needs in check. He admired her for that.

Her relationship with Damian was confusing, but Hades knew it was also part of the walls she had constructed around her. Damian was part of her protection. Both physically and emotionally. She could use him as an excuse not to get close to anyone else. She could feign love for Damian, but Hades knew their relationship was based on mutual necessity. Damian needed her like a pet needed an owner. For care and affection. And he figured Kat needed him for the same reasons, so she could care and feel.

Hades hoped he would have the chance to make her feel something for him. He knew she desired him. In the anticipation of mutual pleasure, he knew she would spread her legs for him. But Hades wanted more. Surprisingly, he wanted much more.

Hades stumbled once more and went down to a knee. While he pushed back up and righted himself, an angry roar sounded all around him. He squinted into the horizon. He could see a black wavering figure moving toward him. A cloud of dust sprayed up behind the shape.

Kat.

She was here to rescue him. Hades laughed. How absurd to have to be rescued. Never in his fifteen years of hunting had he needed to be rescued. Now a woman, another hunter, once his sworn rival, was racing on her steel horse to save him. He laughed hard again. The laughter turned to hoarse coughs and he stumbled. This time he went down hard on his hands and knees.

He crawled forward and then scrambled to his feet. His head spun and he thought he might throw up, except he knew there was nothing in his stomach except bile. His throat began to burn as his gorge rose. Closing his eyes in earnest, he took several wobbly steps forward.

Just as he took another step, he felt a hand on his shoulder. There was no ground beneath his foot. He reeled forward and then felt himself pulled backward. He fell on his ass. Opening his eyes, Hades saw the canyon spread out before him and his feet near the edge of the cliff. He shook his head and glanced over his shoulder. Kat sat upon her bike, her hand still gripping the collar of his cloak, her knuckles white with strain.

"Were you going to fly across to the other side?"

Hades tried to smile. His lips were sore and cracked, but he managed to lift the corners. "Maybe."

"Get on this damn bike."

"Happily."

Slowly Hades pushed himself up to his feet. He held on to Kat—or she hung on to him, he wasn't sure which. After straddling the bike, he pushed himself close to her, wrapping his arms around her waist. He squeezed her tightly. She felt like heaven in his arms.

"Sorry, am I squeezing too tight?"

Kat's mouth twitched at the corners. "No, not at all." She revved the bike and raced toward the shelter.

10

Hades had almost died. She had been certain she couldn't get to him in time.

When she saw where Hades had been walking, Kat lost all her breath. She had pulled on the gas but doubted she'd make it before he stepped off the cliff. She got there just in time, grabbing him roughly by the collar. As she felt him fall forward, she thought he would pull her off with him. Then she yanked back with all she had.

When he had glanced at her, with a stunned and giddy face, she had felt like crying. She had not felt that sensation in more years than she had fingers. The last time she had cried was at the bedside of her dying sister; the last one in her family to succumb to the deadly Avian Flu.

As they raced along to the refuge, Kat attributed these feelings to her baked brain. The sun had a powerful effect on one's thoughts. Heatstroke, from which she was sure they were all suffering, could produce hallucinations and feelings of panic and sorrow. She hoped, once they were safely in shade and rehydrated, that the feelings would dissipate. She had gone on so long without any emotions that she would be at a loss as to what to do with them.

The green oasis rose in front of them. A few more minutes and they would be safely in shade and able to rest. Kat felt a sense of relief wash over her and she smiled.

The bike sputtered and jolted forward. Kat swore as steam rose from the tank. Revving the engine, she pushed the machine faster. They were almost there. If she could just prod them a little faster. She pulled on the gas. The bike wobbled dangerously but she righted it. Just a little more.

It sputtered again. The speedometer revved and then the bike began to slow. Kat pulled on the gas again, but the motorcycle didn't respond. It was done. This was the farthest it was going to go. They rolled to a stop.

"Did we make it?" Hades asked, his head slumped forward on her back.

"No." Kat kicked out the stand.

Hades raised his head. Their refuge lay spread out before them, but it was still a couple of clicks away.

Kat dismounted from the bike and helped Hades off. She swore and kicked the bike. It fell onto its side with a creaking whine. "Piece of shit! We were so close!"

Hades grabbed her arm and pulled her forward. "We're close enough. C'mon."

They stumbled forward, clinging to each other for support. As Kat concentrated on putting one foot in front of the other, she wondered if she could make it. She had never felt so tired and defeated before in her life. She giggled to herself. Shit, they weren't even near the city yet. They were only halfway to their goal. If this was just the beginning of their trials on this journey, they would not make it. Not any of them.

Turning slightly, she watched as Hades plodded forward. His head was slumped again, his chin touching his chest, and he seemed to drag his feet with each step. He stumbled once and nearly pulled her down. She helped him straighten up, and they continued to plod on.

"I don't hate you," she confessed, not sure why it mattered that he know. Perhaps because she didn't want to die without making a connection with him.

Hades glanced over at her, a small smile playing on his cracked lips. "I know."

She returned his smile. The man had an uncanny ability to pull at her. Her heart did not feel so heavy when he was near. He was the first man to make her feel more than a sense of obligation or affection.

Damian didn't make her feel giddy. Damian didn't make her heart pound so hard in her chest that it felt like bursting. He didn't make her feel frustration and respect all at the same time.

Hades made her feel like a woman, not a warrior.

After stumbling again, Hades went down, pulling her with him. The weight of his body propelled her to the ground. Her body twisted and she landed hard on her back. A grunt of pain expelled from his mouth as Hades landed heavily on top of her. Any breath she had left was pushed out of her lungs by the impact.

Both motionless, they tried to gain their breath and their wits. Finally Kat was able to take in air regularly. She opened her eyes and stared into the side of Hades's head. His face was buried in her neck. She could barely feel his hot breath on her throat.

"Get up, Hades."

"I can't," he managed to croak.

"Yes, you can."

"I don't want to move. I don't want to ever move again," he said quietly.

"Hades, you asshole, get up. I refuse to die like this, trapped underneath you."

"Would it help if you were on top?"

"It might." Kat began to laugh. She couldn't help it. The ridiculousness of the situation overwhelmed her. And Hades's fondness for jokes made it seem even more ridiculous. He had the gift of making any dire situation bearable, even laughable.

Raising his head, Hades seemed to gaze down at her. She wished she could see his eyes through the tint of the goggles.

"If I was a normal guy and you were a normal girl, this might be the best time to talk about our feelings for each other."

"But we aren't normal, are we?"

Hades shook his head and leaned down, stopping a mere breath away from her lips. "Promise me one thing, and I'll get us to safety."

"What?" She breathed heavily, wanting him desperately to press his mouth to hers.

"That when we're safe and healed, you'll let me lay on top of you again."

Kat chuckled, her lips cracking open. "I promise."

With incredible strength, Hades pushed up with his hands and pulled Kat to her feet. They stood facing each other. Hades leaned down and put his arms around her waist. He picked her up and swung her over his shoulder.

Kat shrieked. "What are you doing?"

"Saving us both."

He wrapped an arm around her legs to keep her still and then started to walk. His legs wobbled at first. Then he gained speed. Soon Hades pushed all his might and strength into his limbs, and he began to run.

Kat hung on as Hades ran. She clamped her eyes shut against the well of tears that threatened to erupt. She was unnerved at the reserves of power and survival Hades still had left in him. It was no wonder the man was a legend, revered like a god of old.

It was now that Kat prayed to her gods of old. She never prayed. Never felt the need to, or the point. But as she felt her energy drain and her will flutter like the wind, she needed to do something. She didn't make any promises of being a better person or helping those in need, for she knew she would never keep them. But she did make an oath that she would release Damian from her care and make sure he had at least the tools to make a life of his own. A happy one, where love could find him whole and receptive.

She squeezed her eyes tighter as the first tear slipped out and ran down her forehead, evaporating into her dirty matted hair.

"We made it. We made it," Hades whispered, his voice hoarse and cracked.

He stopped and fell to his knees, bringing Kat forward and dropping her onto the soft carpet of grass. He collapsed face first into the semicool shade of the trees. Kat opened her eyes and stared at the waving leaves in the overhanging branches of the big oak trees. She raised her hand and waved back. Grinning, she let her hand fall to the ground. They were going to live.

She closed her eyes and fell away into a deep, dark chasm.

11

Kat's eyes fluttered open as cool, sweet water dripped over her lips. She parted them and let the refreshing liquid drip into her mouth. She stuck out her tongue for more. She was not disappointed as more water slowly dribbled into her open, eager mouth. Pain shot through her as she swallowed. Her throat, withered into a piece of dried meat, barely opened for the liquid, and she choked.

"Slowly."

Kat opened her eyes fully and stared at the person kneeling next to her. She quickly closed them and then opened them again. She must be dreaming.

The man crouched down next to her was shiny and pale. He was bald and completely hairless. Even the area above his dark blue eyes was smooth. He wore no clothes except a short white wrap of cloth at his crotch. It covered him, but barely.

Kat tried to raise herself. "Who . . ."

Considering his lanky frame, he pushed her back down with substantial force. "Do not waste your energy. I am no threat to you."

He put the canteen to her mouth. "Drink some more. The water is sugar-laced. It will help you gather your strength."

Kat took in more; this time she swallowed without choking. The liquid tasted like honey, a taste she had not experienced since she was a child.

"My name is Nemo."

"Where are . . ."

"Your friends are being looked after."

Kat turned her head and saw Hades being attended to by another man identical to this one. Hades was still unconscious.

"Your other female is . . . is of the darkness. We are not sure if we can help her."

"Is she still alive?"

"Yes, but barely. What she needs we are not willing to give."

Kat nodded. She understood, for she would not willingly give up her blood for Darquiel either. Closing her eyes again, she thought of the oath she'd made in her prayer. For Damian and his happiness. This certainly could not be part of the bargain. She would help him in other ways.

She swore softly to herself. "I will . . . feed her."

Nemo appeared surprised. "She means that much to you?"

"No, but the man lying next to her does."

Nemo nodded as he helped her sit up. Her head spun and she nearly passed out. He pressed his hand to the nape of her neck. She noticed the thin skin between his fingers, like the webbing of a duck's foot. But it was cool and comforting, like a cold compress. Her nausea quickly passed.

She was able to get to her hands and knees and she crawled to where Darquiel was sprawled. A bald and shiny female crouched next to her, but not too close. She was naked except for a similar strip of cloth around her crotch. She scrambled backward as Kat neared.

"It's all right, Naiad," Nemo said as he touched the woman on the shoulder. "She has come to feed this . . . girl."

Naiad nodded and stilled her movements.

Kat sat down next to Darquiel and gazed down at her prone form. Her skin was almost translucent. She could clearly see the veins in her face and hands. They were no longer blue, but a deeper color, almost black. Carefully Kat studied her. She stared at her chest until she could see the slight lift as her lungs filled. Kat's gorge rose while she stared at the girl.

Nemo crouched next to her, concern furrowing his brow. "Are you sure?"

"No." Kat contemplated Damian. He was still unconscious and lay close to Darquiel. He looked at peace, his face slack and line free. But Kat knew if he woke and found Darquiel dead, he would not go on. Somehow they were linked now that Darquiel had taken his blood. Her death might just catapult Damian into a self-destructive downspin that could possibly force Kat to defend herself and end his life.

Uncertain that she could live with that guilt, Kat reached down and unsheathed the small dagger from her ankle. She raised her hand above Darquiel's mouth. With one quick swipe of her blade, Kat's palm split open and thick red blood oozed out. Small drops landed on Darquiel's mouth. Soon her lips were crimson with Kat's blood and some ran down over her chin.

Darquiel's lips parted. Kat didn't think she had awakened, but assumed her predatory instincts kicked in. Her throat moved as she swallowed the liquid. Kat kept her hand over Darquiel's gaping mouth until dark spots clouded her eyes. She withdrew her hand and closed it into a tight fist.

"I have fulfilled my oath," she said quietly.

Naiad moved next to Kat and handed her a thin strip of cloth. The girl tipped her head as Kat took it and wrapped it tightly around her wound.

"Hopefully that will be enough to keep her alive," Nemo commented as he helped Kat stand.

Kat wobbled and he held her firm. "You know what she is?"

"Yes, we have dealt with her kind before."

"Where . . . ?"

"Enough questions right now. We must get you to our village. There you can be properly cared for."

"Ahhhh!" Hades sat up and opened his eyes.

The man attending him yelped and scrambled backward. Everyone else jumped.

Hades turned to find Kat. His brow furrowed when he noticed Nemo hanging on tightly to her arm. Hades pushed up with his hands.

"It's all right," Kat assured him. "They're here to help."

Hades blinked rapidly and returned to his position on the ground. Bringing up a hand to his head, he rubbed at his brow. "I have a killer headache."

"The sun nearly fried your brain. Of course you have a headache," the other man commented sarcastically.

"Triton, there is no need to be rude," Nemo berated.

"What were you people doing out there? No sane, rational person would go out on the wastelands in full day," Triton asked, a trace of annoyance in his voice.

Nemo held up his hand. "We will save our questions, too, until we are safely at our village." Nemo glanced down at Hades. "Do you think you can stand?"

Hades nodded. He sat up again, this time slowly.

"Help him, Triton," Nemo commanded.

The other shiny man stood and held out his webbed hand. Hades looked at it a moment and then up to Triton's face. He took his hand. Triton pulled him to his feet.

"We will carry your other male, but you will have to carry the other. We will not touch her if we don't have to."

"Hades, do you think you could carry her?"

He nodded. "If you tied her onto my back. She weighs next to nothing." He stumbled over to where Darquiel lay.

Nemo let go of Kat as she bent forward to heft Darquiel up. Still very weak, she couldn't lift Darquiel high enough. Kat tried again, to no avail. Sweat popped out on her forehead and upper lip. She felt like fainting again. She glanced around at the shiny people. They retreated and watched Kat and Hades struggle in silence.

"Could one of you help me?" Kat snarled, exhausted from trying to lift Darquiel.

Nemo shook his head. "She is from the darkness. Their clan have raided our village and stolen our people. We cannot help those that harm us."

"She may be from the 'darkness,' as you say, but she is not part of that clan," Kat explained. "She came from Burnsbow, a village far from here in the southern plains. She escaped from the city years ago, and is now our guide back in. She will not harm you."

Nemo eyed her questioningly. Kat couldn't believe she was sticking up for Darquiel. Only a day ago she was ready to shoot her where she stood. Later she might regret this, but now she needed to get the girl onto Hades's back.

Nemo continued to stare. She could see that he was thinking. Nodding, he stepped forward. With both their efforts, they managed to secure Darquiel onto Hades's shoulders.

Triton picked up Damian with ease and slung him over his shoulder. Nemo steadied Kat with a firm hand on her arm. Hades shuffled up next to them, Darquiel hanging off his back. Naiad led the way into the trees. They followed the strange woman into the woods. They had no choice.

12

As they walked through the thick trees, Kat wandered how such growth was possible. She could not ever recall seeing green so bright, so lush. Flowers even grew on the forest floor. She had not seen one outside a book. There were colors she had no idea nature could make. While she gaped around in awe, Nemo gave her a reassuring smile.

It was not long before they emerged from the trees and into a large clearing. A clearing that turned into a busy, vibrant village. Two shiny men armed with spears greeted them as they stepped out of the woods.

Kat gazed around in wonder as more shiny men and women appeared. Some came out of surrounding buildings made from wood. Buildings with wide porches and overhangs, providing much needed shade. Looking around, she noticed that most of the village was covered by overhangs or by thatched canopies held up by thick poles buried in the ground. They were very well protected from the harsh rays of the unforgiving sun.

As Kat gazed around at all the shiny pale faces, she felt nausea rise in her throat once more. "Who are you?"

"We will share our stories once you are rested and nourished." Nemo regarded his kin, searching the faces. "Leucothea?"

A petite young woman parted the crowd. She was clothed like the rest, with only a cloth wrap around her waist, but she stuck out like a sore thumb. She had long, chestnut-brown hair and matching eyebrows.

She came quickly to Nemo's side and bowed her head.

"You will help me aid our visitors," Nemo instructed the girl.

"Yes, Nemo."

Leucothea led the way through the village to a large wood longhouse. Inside the house were several beds with wooden frames, lined up against the wall. Triton set Damian down on one. Kat and Nemo untied Darquiel from Hades's back and set her down on a bed in the corner. Both Kat and Hades found beds of their own.

Leucothea bustled around them like a flighty bird. She knelt down at Kat's feet and began to untie her boots. Kat pulled away her foot.

"It's all right. Leucothea will help you undress," Nemo offered.

"I don't need help," Kat argued, her eyes heavy. "I just need to sleep."

"You need to lower your body temperature or you may not wake from your sleep."

Kat glanced at Damian's still form. "You mean he might not wake up?"

Nemo shrugged. "I do not know. All I know is that we can prevent that for the both of you. If you quit being stubborn, that is."

Hades shrugged like a man numbed by too much alcohol and then began to shed his clothes. He struggled with his cloak, and Leucothea helped him. As he tried to wrestle off his shirt, she aided him with his boots.

Kat stripped off her goggles and watched as Hades wrestled with his clothing. He looked at her and grinned. "C'mon, babe. Let's get naked." Then he began to giggle like a little boy.

Kat shook her head. "Will you be able to fix him? I don't think I could stand it if his brains are fried."

"If we can get him into the tub right away. The sun can turn the healthiest of folk into babbling idiots," Nemo replied.

"I noticed," Kat scoffed.

Hades finally managed to rip off his shirt. Underneath he was all rippled muscle. Kat marveled at the pure beauty of his form. Like a statue carved from granite, chiseled with deft skill and artistic flair. With what little saliva she had, she found her mouth watering as he reclined against the mattress and let the girl remove his boots. He glanced over at her and grinned, knowing full well what she was staring at.

"Like the package, babe?"

Kat sniffed. "Yeah, the packaging is great. It's what's inside I'm beginning to doubt."

"You can't doubt this," he stated as he stood up and unbuttoned his pants.

Tearing her eyes from Hades's strip show, she glanced at Nemo, who was supervising all of this. He had an amused expression on his face. "What's funny?"

"You are a mated couple?"

"Hell, no," Kat snorted.

"Well, you should be." And with that he walked over to Hades and held him up as he struggled with his pants.

Kat reluctantly turned and watched as his pants came off. As her eyes widened, she had no doubt whatsoever of his packaging. She remembered all too well when his arousal had been pressed like steel against her lower back. While she gazed at him, she took in a ragged breath. Even when not aroused, the man was a marvel to take in.

Once he was completely naked, Nemo and Leucothea helped

him over to the large wooden tub that had been filled with water. Kat stared at his ass as he passed her. She had once come across a video box that proclaimed to be about buns of steel. It wasn't until she read the back of the box that she realized they were talking about the muscles of the buttocks and not rock-hard pastry. Now, as she gazed at Hades, she understood what they were talking about. He definitely had buns of steel.

"You're looking at my ass, aren't you?"

"No," she answered indignantly.

Leucothea smiled shyly at Kat. "He probably won't remember any of this later."

"Then, yes, I was staring at your ass, Hades, and your cock. You are the most incredible-looking man I have ever seen, and I desperately want to fuck you."

Hades just smiled and nodded. "I knew it." He glanced down at Leucothea. "I knew it."

"Of course you did." She patted him on the arm as if he were a child. "Now take a big step into the tub."

Hades raised his leg and put it into the water. He flinched. "It's cold."

"It will help you cool down," Nemo explained.

"It's too cold. I don't wanna." Hades stepped out of the tub.

"You'll feel better once you're in, I promise," Leucothea coaxed.

"I'm not going in. It's too cold."

Kat sighed. "Hades, you're acting like a child."

He scrunched up his face in indignation. "No, I'm not."

"Yes, you are."

"Am not."

"Are, too."

"Am not."

"Are, too."

"Am not, infinity." Then he stuck out his tongue.

Kat shook her head. "Just push him in."

"Oh, no, we can't do that," Nemo objected. "That would be a shock to his system. Who knows what would happen."

Kat stood up. "Fine, I'll do it." She rushed at them and pushed Hades.

Pinwheeling his arms, Hades teetered backward toward the large tub. As he reached out for purpose, he found it in Kat. Grasping her shirt, he pulled her down with him. They landed with a tremendous splash. Water spouted everywhere and over everything, including Nemo and Leucothea.

As they submerged, Kat lost her breath. The water gripped her with its icy tendrils. She felt as though there should be steam coming off them, like a hot frying pan under a water tap.

They both came up spewing water and obscenities.

"Fuck! I told you it was cold!" Hades hollered.

"Don't be a baby," Kat said through chattering teeth. She sat up so she was not pressed intimately against his naked body. So that no part of her touched him, she moved to the other side of the tub and pulled up her legs. She was too acutely aware of his fine physical form.

"That's easy for you to say, you're not naked."

"I know." She made the mistake of smiling.

Hades grabbed her legs and pulled her forward. She quickly went under the water. As she bumped the back of her head on the side, the leather strap on her eye patch broke.

When she resurfaced, spurting water, and rubbed at her face, she instantly noticed the absence of her patch. She glanced down in the water and saw it floating on top. She glanced up at Hades. He was staring at her. Pity shone in his wide eyes. Kat grabbed the patch and scrambled out of the tub.

"Kat!" Hades pushed up.

Nemo put a gentle hand on his shoulder and pushed back down. "Your body temperature is still high. You can do no one any good if you don't get well."

Hades shivered but sunk down into the water.

"She will forgive you," Nemo affirmed.

"How do you know?"

"Because I have three wives."

Leucothea rushed to Kat's side. "You need to get out of these wet clothes."

"I'll be fine," she said as she shivered uncontrollably.

"No, you won't. You will die. I have seen it happen."

Kat looked down at Leucothea's innocent face. "Fine, but I want privacy."

Leucothea nodded and rushed over to the wall. She picked up a folded, thatched divider and brought it over to Kat's bed, setting it up around them so they could not be seen.

Kat's whole body shook violently. She could not stop her shaking. With Leucothea's aid, Kat removed her wet, sopping clothing, slinging them over the divider to dry. Leucothea took the broken eye patch from Kat's trembling hands.

"I will fix it for you."

Kat nodded, too tired to do much else.

"But you should not be ashamed of your marks," Leucothea proclaimed. "You are obviously a mighty warrior, and you should display your battle wounds with honor."

"I am no warrior."

"You are modest. But the gods did not send you to us if you were not."

"Leucothea, mind your tongue," Nemo chided from behind the divider.

"My apologies, Nemo."

Leucothea wrapped Kat in a large wool blanket and laid her down on the bed. She rushed away and returned with a teapot and two cups on a wooden tray. Steam rose from the cups.

She sat down next to Kat's bed and lifted the cup to her lips. Kat took small, tentative sips. The tea was hot, strong, and tasted mildly of herbs. Kat did not enjoy the flavor, but she knew the brew would help her. When she had taken the last sip, she could feel the warmth spread in her body. Her shakes quieted to mild shivers.

"Who are you people?" Kat asked.

"We are the Nerieds, the People of the Ocean."

"I didn't know you existed."

Leucothea smiled. "And I did not know of your existence. But now that you are here, we can know of each other."

"Leucothea, help me with the giant," Nemo asked.

She bowed her head to Kat and scrambled out from the divider to help Nemo with Hades. Kat heard the water slosh as Hades was helped out of the tub. She saw shadows pass behind the divider as they walked him to the next bed. Kat moved slightly to glance down past her bed. She watched as they laid Hades, also wrapped in a wool blanket, down on the bed. He was shivering worse than she had been. Leucothea crouched down and offered him the same tea.

Kat could feel her eyes grow heavy. Her body had stopped convulsing and she almost felt normal. The skin on her face and hands still felt raw and sore, but with time she knew that would pass. She closed her eyes and let herself drift into the warm embrace of the dark behind her eyes. The sensation felt just like floating on water.

13

The dark. It was all-consuming. Oppressive and ominous. Not a pinprick of light shone through.

Hades stood immobile in the dark. His own heavy breathing invaded his ears. He felt like the dark was touching him, caressing him in his most secret areas. He shuddered with revulsion from the intimate touch. Tendrils of panic wrapped themselves tightly around his stomach and chest and squeezed him in a vice like grip. He could hardly breathe.

An unpleasant odor invaded his nostrils. He knew the smell. It was metallic and sharp. He took a step forward in the pitch dark and his foot slid on the floor. He knew if there was light, and if he looked down, he would see the ground slicked with blood. His gorge rose.

He knew where the blood came from. He had been here before.

Hades took another step forward. As his feet slipped he reached out for purpose. His hand found something solid and cold and he grasped it to stop from falling. The object moved under his firm hold. Suspended from an unseen ceiling, it swung back and forth.

He moved to get a better grip and his hand slipped over something congealed like jelly. Hades flinched, sensing the nature of it. Bending over, he violently retched on the floor.

Laughter echoed throughout the dark. A strange and hollow sound, menacing and mocking.

"Welcome back, Hades. Do you think you can save her this time?"

Spotlights flashed on, illuminating a dank and empty room made of cement. Under the light, a figure hung by his or her hands from a chain suspended from the high ceiling. Other bodies hung suspended around the room. Each with their own blood pools beneath.

The figure in the spotlight was naked and definitely female, from the flare of hip and round buttocks. Her back was slender but roped with muscle. Weeping, angry welts marred her skin. She had been whipped numerous times. Blood pooled beneath her swinging body.

The body began to swing around.

Hades closed his eyes. Although he already knew who it was, he didn't want to see. He opened them just as she turned to face him.

Kat.

More crimson slashes marked her chest and belly. Blood slowly dribbled down her legs.

Hades moaned. "No!"

Kat's eyes opened. She smiled at him. Tiny pointed fangs peeked out between her swollen lips.

"Save me," she whispered.

Hades bolted from his sleep and sat straight up in his bed. Trying to calm himself, he took in two gulping breaths. Cold, stinging sweat dripped into his eyes. He rubbed his hands over his head and face, hoping to erase the images.

They still lingered viciously in the dark recesses of his mind.

He swung his feet around and off the bed to glance around the room, remembering where he was and what had happened. His eyes rested on Kat, who slept in the next bed. Still swaddled in the wool blanket, she seemed to be at peace. He turned away and buried his head in his hands. At least he knew one piece of the puzzle. The woman he had been dreaming about lay a mere two feet away.

He raised his head and looked around at the other beds. He glanced briefly at Damian, who still slept, and rested his stare on Darquiel. She lay on her back, her hands inactive on her chest, appearing dead and already cradled in her coffin.

He wondered, not for the first time, if they were being led into a trap.

"Oh, you're awake." Nemo entered the room, a tray in his hands.

"Where the fuck are we?"

"And lucid. Thank the gods." He set down the tray on a nearby table. "We weren't sure if you would regain your senses." Nemo handed Hades a cup of steaming tea. "Drink this and I will tell you all you wish to know."

Hades glanced fleetingly into the cup. The liquid was brown and thick. He sniffed it. The smell was horrid, like rotten fish. Putting the cup to his lips, he drained it in two big gulps.

Nemo's eyes widened in surprise.

Hades handed him back the cup. "Talk."

"What do you remember?"

"Baking."

"Well, we found you on the outskirts of our village, in the grove. How you even managed to survive that long in the wastelands is beyond me."

Hades glanced briefly at Kat.

Nemo caught the look. "A formidable woman, to say the least."

Nodding, Hades's attention returned to Nemo. "Where is 'here'?"

"You are in the Neried village of Atlantis, on the pacific side of the ocean. I am Nemo, the tribe's Chieftain."

Leucothea entered the room and smiled. She stood next to Nemo. "You are awake."

Hades studied her, taking in her pert bare breasts and shiny pale skin. "How is it you can walk around exposed to the sun? Are you mutants?"

Leucothea flinched as if struck and gasped aloud.

Nemo put a comforting hand on her shoulder. "It's all right." He patted her reassuringly. "Yes, Hades, we are mutations of sorts. Our ancestors came from the ocean when the land was submerged after the Great War. They learned to survive in the harshness of the scorched Earth, so near to water that could not be consumed or used to grow vegetation. They learned to harness the ocean, and adapted to its environment. Our bodies now have a natural ability to cool itself from the inside out, and we can swim underwater longer and faster, like a porpoise."

"Is that why you're shiny? Like a fish?"

Nemo brushed a hand over his arm. It came away wet with a jellylike substance. "We developed an ointment that protects us from the blazing rays of the sun." He reached out toward Hades with his slick hand.

Hades flinched and pulled away from his advances.

"It also heals already burned skin."

Hades halted and brought a hand up to his face. He touched his cheeks and chin gently. They were sore. Flakes of skin were already peeling away. He looked up at Nemo. He could tell the man was an honest one. It showed in the way he held himself, and in the way the girl regarded him. He was obviously revered as a leader. Hades would have to trust him. If they were to get well and continue on their journey, he had no other choice.

Hades nodded curtly. With care, Nemo rubbed the cool ointment onto his face. The moment the substance touched his skin, he felt relief. His skin no longer throbbed. He could move his jaw without fearing his flesh would crack open.

"Bring some for her," Hades said, motioning toward Kat.

"We have enough for everyone. Except you will have to put it on your other female yourself."

Hades glanced quickly at Darquiel and then back to Nemo. "What are you scared of?"

"She is unclean. Just having her in our midst is insult enough. We have done all we will to aid her." Nemo motioned to Leucothea. "Bring the ointment and treat the other two."

"Yes, Nemo."

"I will leave you now to rest."

"I have other questions."

"They will have to wait." Nemo turned and walked out of the room.

Hades watched as Leucothea smeared the clear ointment on Damian's face, hands, and any skin that had been exposed. He moaned in his sleep but did not wake. She then went to aid Kat.

"Why are you afraid of the girl?" he asked her.

Leucothea continued to smooth the gel over Kat's face and didn't meet Hades's gaze. "The Dark Dwellers raid our village. They take our people from us. Those people never come back. We know what is done to them down in the darkness. Last time they came, Kele, one of Nemo's wives, was taken."

"How long ago?"

Leucothea shrugged. "Maybe a moon turn ago."

She turned down the blanket off Kat's shoulders. As she pulled out Kat's arms, Hades caught a glimpse of Kat's breasts. They were pale, round, and perfect. He closed his eyes and sighed. In his mind he still saw them torn and bleeding.

When he heard Kat moan, he opened his eyes and watched as her eyelids fluttered open. He stared into them, both green and white, without looking away. She was the most breathtaking woman he had ever seen. And he silently feared for her and for himself.

"What did I miss?" Her voice was raw and hoarse.

Hades smiled at her. "Nothing yet, darling. The party's just starting."

Kat rolled onto her back and stretched. Her limbs and muscles were stiff and sore but relatively workable—surprising for what they had been through. She reached up and touched her face. It felt tingly and cool.

"What's this shit?"

Leucothea stood and put her hands on her hips indignantly. "It is not shit. It is a salve I make that helps soothe and protect the skin."

Kat put up her hand in defense. "Sorry. No offense intended."

The girl lost her indignant look and smiled. "No need. Most people are scared of what they do not understand."

Kat glanced at Hades and cocked a brow.

He shrugged. "Don't ask me, I just woke up, too."

"How long were we out?"

"Eighteen hours about," Leucothea answered.

Gathering the blanket to her chest, Kat sat up and swung her feet around to set them on the wooden floor. She closed her eyes and bowed her head a moment, still feeling dizzy and off balance.

"How do you feel?" Hades asked.

"Like I got too much sun."

He chuckled. "Me, too."

"I will get you both something to eat. Your strength will come back, gradually." Leucothea turned and left the room.

Kat touched her face again. "Is this why they are shiny and pale?"

Hades nodded. "It blocks the sun's rays. They also have a natural ability to cool themselves from the inside out."

"I wonder if they'll give us some when we leave."

"Let's hope so."

Kat gazed around the wide room. It looked like a hospital, with the beds lined up along the wall; the tub in the corner; and tables lined with bowls, small cylindrical containers containing different substances. Nothing Kat could identify. She supposed that was what this place was, the village hospital. But with the thatched roof and the wooden walls, she imagined this place more likely on the beach, like a holiday cabin.

"Where are our clothes?" Kat asked.

"Don't know."

"Our weapons?"

"Don't know that either."

Kat eyed Hades, her brow lifted in question. "We're at a disadvantage."

"That we are."

"I don't like being vulnerable."

"Neither do I, but there's not much we can do about it now. We were in no shape to disagree yesterday."

"There's a scalpel on the table over there." She motioned to the small table by the open window.

"Leave it, Kat. These people are no threat to us."

"How can you be sure?"

"They rescued us, nursed us, and now what—they want to harm us? Makes no sense. They could have left us to fry."

"Maybe they want something from us."

Hades looked away from her. He was hiding something.

"Hades?"

He rubbed a hand over his head. "It's possible we are here for a reason."

Before Kat could question him further, Leucothea returned with a food tray. She set it down on the floor between the beds and sat down beside it. On the tray were slices of some kind of fruit. The sweet smell wafted up Kat's nose. Her stomach growled in desperate response.

Leucothea smiled and handed both her and Hades a small clay plate. "These will help you heal."

Hades touched a thin orange wedge. The corners of his mouth lifted. "It's an orange."

"Yes, we grow them in abundance."

Kat picked up a wedge and sniffed it. The smell made her mouth water. She had never eaten an orange before. She had heard of them and had seen pictures in a book when she was a child. But her family had never had the kind of money that was needed to buy such rarities.

She put it in her mouth and bit down. Sweet, tangy juices squirted on her tongue. Closing her eyes, she savored the glorious flavor.

"I had an orange once," Hades said as he chewed slowly on a piece, staring at the floor. "I must have been around ten. My dad and I were at the market, trading beef for vegetables and other things we needed. We came across this old beggar. He asked us for some money. My dad gave him some coins. He was generous, my dad. The old man gave us an orange. It had a few brown spots on it, but we didn't care. After our marketing, we sat by the old creek and shared that orange. Best damn thing I ever tasted."

As she listened to the story, Kat stopped chewing. She could see the regret and longing on his face, and wondered why. From his stories of his past, she could tell that he had had a good childhood, a good family. She pondered what had changed in his life that would bring that expression of hurt and sorrow to his handsome face.

Granting him the respect and privacy he deserved for his

painful past, she moved her gaze to Leucothea. The girl was watching Hades with rapt attention.

"Why is it that you have hair and the others don't?"

Leucothea turned her innocent face toward Kat. "I have not undergone my Rite of Passage yet." She smiled and seemed to bounce on her knees. "But I have passed my eighteenth lunar cycle, and it is now my time."

"What is the Rite of Passage?"

"You will see. That's if you will honor me by attending this evening?" She looked at both of them, eagerness on her face.

"Sure. We're not going anywhere," Hades answered as he popped the last of his orange into his mouth.

Leucothea bounced to her feet. "I'm pleased to hear this." She stooped to pick up the tray. "I have to go now and start preparations, but I will send someone to help you get ready." She bowed and bounded out of the room.

Kat scoffed, "Like hell I'm going."

"Relax, Kat. Could be culturally stimulating."

"I don't give a shit about culture. I want to get going."

Hades reclined against the wall and closed his eyes. "Hell will be waiting for us. Let's enjoy this little piece of heaven for as long as it lasts. Besides, the two of them aren't going anywhere."

Kat swallowed the last of her orange as she stared at Hades. He wasn't telling her something. She saw a flicker of doubt on his face before he leaned back. Doubt or . . . possibly fear. But what could Hades possibly fear?

14

Kat and Hades had both slept on and off for the rest of the day. After Kat had demanded a robe from Leucothea, she got up from her bed and checked on Damian. Through the night he had moaned often but made no sign of waking.

Sitting at his side, she brushed his hair from his sweaty brow and murmured to him. Movement gave her pause and she glanced up to see Hades watching her. "Do you mind?"

"No."

Kat shifted her gaze from his intense stare and back to Damian's crinkled face. Dipping a finger into a bowl of sweetened water, she trailed it along his lips. They parted in response and she was able to dribble a small amount into his mouth.

"Do you love him?" Hades asked.

She sighed. "Not the way you mean."

"Have you ever loved . . . the way I mean?"

"No."

"Could you?"

Kat's eyes lifted to his then, the implication of the question evident on his face. Though he leaned against the wall, his demeanor relaxed, the look in his eyes was intense. She could feel the weight of it on her, feeling its way over her, into her.

"With so much death and destruction in this world, why would one want to?" she asked, returning her attention to Damian, hoping Hades would let the conversation end.

Before Hades could respond, two female Nerieds came into the room to prepare them for the upcoming ceremony. They both carried white strips of cloth hung over their arms.

"I am not wearing this," Kat exclaimed for the second time. She had a short cloth wrapped around her generous hips, like the villagers, and a thin halter wrapped around her breasts.

"At least they gave you the halter." Hades smiled as he took in her barely there attire. "You could have been walking around bare-breasted like the rest of the tribe."

Kat resisted the urge to punch him. He was grinning at her like a fool. But damn if his smile didn't make her feel warm, especially in her intimate parts. Besides, he didn't look too bad in the short wrap the Nerieds had dressed him in. It left nothing to the imagination and outlined his endowment.

She turned to one of the Nerieds. "Where are my clothes? I'll wear those to the ceremony."

"I am sorry, Katarina, but tradition demands that you wear the tribal uniform," the youngest Neried explained.

Kat sucked in a breath. "What did you just call me?"

"Katarina. Is this not your name? Leucothea told us this, that you muttered it during your restless sleep." The girl bowed her head in shame.

"No, it's fine." Kat could feel Hades staring at her. She turned. "What?"

"Katarina?"

"Yeah, so?" She put her hand on her hip indignantly.

"It's . . . a beautiful name," assured Hades.

Kat smiled. She didn't want his compliment to move her, but it did.

"Too bad your mother didn't realize what a hellion you'd turn out to be."

Kat's smile faded. His mocking remark stung her in places she didn't realize had any feeling, like her heart. Damn him! Damn him for making her feel things she had no business feeling. Damn him for making her crave compliments and soft looks. Damn him for making her want to say that, yes, she could love. Yes, she desperately wanted to.

Closing her hand into a tight fist, she punched Hades in the mouth. He stumbled back, his face a mask of shock. Blood dribbled from his cut lip.

"Oh, she knew," Kat retorted.

The two Nerieds watched in stunned silence.

Kat turned to them and smiled innocently. "Shall we?"

They bowed and led the way out of the room and into the sultry night.

Kat and Hades followed the Nerieds down a path through the trees that eventually opened up onto the beach. The ocean spread out in front of them like a great big blue blanket.

As Kat gazed over its enormity, she sucked in a breath. She had seen pictures of the ocean but she never thought it would be so beautiful, so tranquil. She had images of a great raging titan of water forever foaming and swirling, waiting for the next opportunity to swallow the entire Earth. While she watched the gentle swells and waves caress the soft sand, she realized how wrong she had been.

Glancing at Hades, she noticed the same wonder on his face. Wanting to share this moment with someone, she smiled at him. He returned her look and reached for her hand, squeezing it gently.

She didn't resist the touch, nor did she pull away. His hand felt warm and comforting in hers.

More of the Neried tribe stepped out of the trees and onto the beach. Soon every man and woman stood in a circle around the soft sand, a stone altar in the center.

When Nemo stepped into the center of the circle, the murmur of the crowd dimmed. "We gather here on this sacred ground this night to celebrate a rite of passage. A passage into age, from child to adult, from girl to woman."

The group parted, and Leucothea stepped into the sacred ring. She was completely naked. Her pale skin shone like pearls in the moonlight. She moved next to Nemo. Smiling at her, he helped her up onto the altar, laying her down on her back on the flat, carved stone.

Kat squeezed Hades's hand and leaned toward him. "I don't think I like this."

"Just wait, it's not what you think."

"How do you know?"

"These are not an aggressive people. They're not sacrificing her to their gods. She's sacrificing something to her descent into adulthood."

"What?" Kat asked, concern making her voice tight.

Hades raised his eyebrow in answer.

"Oh." Kat looked back at the altar as a young man stepped up next to Nemo. He was lean, muscular, and completely naked. His arousal was already evident in his stiffening cock.

Nemo handed him a knife with a white, intricately carved handle.

Kat stepped forward into the circle. Hades pulled her back. "Wait."

The young man stepped up to the altar and took Leucothea's long hair in his hand. He sawed at it, tossing the strands into the ocean. Soon her hair was cropped close to her head. She gazed up at the young man and smiled. He bent down and placed a gentle and soft kiss to her lips.

Another Neried rushed into the circle, carrying a clay bowl. He placed it gently on the altar beside Leucothea, and then departed without pause.

The young man dipped his hands into the bowl. When he lifted them, they were covered in a transparent gel not unlike the substance the Nerieds smothered their skin in for protection.

In rapt awe, Kat watched as he spread the substance over Leucothea's head and massaged it into her scalp. He gently rubbed a finger over each eyebrow. He then dipped his hands back into the bowl. This time he smeared the gel over her arms and up and down her legs, gently and sensuously massaging it into her skin.

A deep throb started to ache in Kat's cunt as she watched the young man dip his hands into the gel and rub it over Leucothea's sex. He smeared it over the coarse hair on her mound and dipped his fingers in between her legs, massaging intimately. Leucothea bowed her back and moaned softly.

Kat glanced up at Hades. He was watching the ceremony intently. Surveying the attendees, Kat noticed that the cloths at the men's waists rose. She glanced down at Hades and noticed he too had a hard-on.

"Interested?"

Her head snapped up, up catching his eye. She saw the barely controlled lust swimming in the dark blue depths.

"Maybe," Kat responded, even as desire swirled low in her belly.

He leered down at her. Kat's knees went weak and her heart pounded so fiercely in her chest that she was sure all could hear it.

"Now be cleansed of your impurities and be born a true Neried." Nemo's voice rose to a tremendous pitch.

Kat turned back to the ceremony as Leucothea descended from the altar and walked hand in hand with the young man into the ocean. They both dived into the swelling waves.

Only moments passed before they emerged from the waters, fingers still entwined together. When Leucothea walked into the light of the moon, Kat noticed that all her hair had vanished. Her head was smooth and bald, as was the mound of her sex.

Drums began to sound. Steady rhythmic sounds resonated over the beach and the circle began to move to the beat. Leucothea and her young man began to sway to the music. Soon he was pressed up behind her, his hands trailing over her body. He gently caressed her breast, while his other hand cupped her sex. Leucothea leaned into him and spread her legs in sweet surrender.

The throb at Kat's center pumped to the rhythm of the drums. Soon it hurt deep inside her sex, pain so exquisite that she moaned, unable to keep her legs together. She spread them apart to ease her ache.

Hades squeezed her hand and pulled her out of the circle.

As soon as they were in the woods, he had her pressed up against a tree. His hands were rough as they yanked and pulled at the flimsy halter covering her breasts. He ripped the material away and satisfied his hunger by lowering his head and sucking one rosy peaked nipple into his eager mouth.

Pleasant sensations vibrated through her body. Groaning, Kat closed her eyes in ecstasy as Hades devoured her pert, throbbing buds. He rolled one between his lips and then gently bit down. Kat cried out and dug her fingers into his powerful back.

He moved his hands down her body and cupped her ass. As he lifted her up into his powerful arms, Kat wrapped her arms around his neck and her legs around his waist. He spun her around and brought her down to the forest floor.

The stones on the ground bit into Kat's back, but she didn't feel them. All she could feel was the sultry heat between her legs and the rock-hard body pressed intimately against her.

Hades ripped away his loincloth and nestled his cock against the soft folds of her sex. With her already wet and open, he pressed into her with ease. Kat raked her nails over his skin when he filled her completely; stretched wide to accommodate him.

As he slid back and forth, Kat moaned loudly in his ear. He felt incredible inside her, filling her emptiness. Emptiness she had been hell-bent on claiming and making her own—a decision she was starting to regret.

Hades licked the side of her neck, moving his mouth over her flesh. He nibbled on her chin and found her eager mouth with his own. Bringing up his hands, he buried them in her hair while they kissed.

Every nerve in her body responded to him. To his touch, to his taste. She moaned into his mouth and nipped hungrily at his lips. She wanted to devour him. Raw animal need consumed her. Something she had not felt before. Not with Damian. Not with anyone. With Hades, it went beyond the physical longing. Deep inside her soul, she yearned for him.

The deep ache in her center scared her. She didn't want to desire like this. It was frightening to her very existence. She had prided herself on being alone. Being strong and independent. The need she felt building inside for Hades would threaten that. Threaten all she had worked for. The wall she had built around her heart quivered under the strain.

Kat wrapped her arms around him and rolled him over onto his back. "Too slow. I have a need for speed." Hades chuckled as she straddled him; his cock still imbedded inside the depths of her sex.

She started to rock on him, slow at first and then gaining her rhythm. As flickers of pleasure surged up her body, she started to pump faster, harder. Slamming herself down onto him. The sounds of flesh against flesh reverberated around them in the trees.

Hades reached up and molded her breasts in his hands, flicking his thumbs over her peaked nipples. He trailed a hand down her torso, caressing her skin to where they joined. His fingers found her wet cleft, cleverly nudging his knuckle against her clit.

Jolts of fervent sensations rang up her body. She could feel her orgasm tightening inside her cunt. It would not take much more to drive her over the edge.

Hades gripped a hand around waist and stilled her motions. "Not so fast. I want to feel every inch of you."

Kat pushed his hand away and slammed herself down hard.

With both hands, Hades encircled her hips, slowing her movement. He lifted her up slowly along his cock, held her still with just the tip of him inside, and then brought her down inch by excruciating inch.

Kat could barely contain herself. All her muscles and nerve endings began to hum and vibrate. His slow, exquisite torture on her insides was sending her spiraling to the edge, hovering in midair. Her cunt contracted around him as her climax slammed into her with an explosive force.

Crying out, she fell forward to bury her head into the warmth of his neck. He wrapped his arms around her and continued to pump his cock, bringing him to orgasm soon after. She could feel every surge of his seed inside her.

Clamping her eyes shut against the tears that welled there, she felt like a dam had burst inside her. Liquid leaked from all her parts as emotions she didn't know she had spilled free.

Hades kissed the side of her neck as his orgasm subsided. She could feel his hot breath on her sensitive skin. By the intake of breath, she could tell he wanted to say something, but instead he resigned himself to kissing her on the cheek and resting his head against hers.

She was relieved for that. She didn't think she could handle any words. The unwanted emotions alone were enough to handle. She definitely couldn't cope with any words that went with them.

15

From the beach, Kat and Hades made their way back to the long, thatched house. The Nerieds still celebrated out on the sand, so the village was near empty and quiet. Hand in hand, they walked in comfortable silence. Kat still felt warm and languid from their lovemaking.

She had expected the sex to be great—mind-blowing actually—but it was the emotions welling in her that she didn't anticipate. With Damian, it had always been uncomplicated and relaxed. She didn't feel jealous when he fucked other women. Kat knew it was only to scratch an itch, and that he would return to her bed the next day. His leash was on a long tether.

But with Hades, everything seemed different and foreign. Kat knew she'd never tolerate a wandering eye or hand from him. Rage filled her just thinking about him with someone else. Unwillingly, she'd branded him. Marked him hers.

In return, he had his mark on her. She could almost feel it seared into her skin like a burn. Without her knowledge, she'd gone ahead and started to fall in love.

Damn treacherous heart!

As Kat entered the makeshift hospital, she pulled Hades through the doorway. She came to an abrupt stop and released his hand. "Damian."

Damian sat in his bed, his feet on the floor, and his head in his hands. He looked up as they neared him. Narrowing his eyes, he shook his head. "I still must be dreaming. I swear, Kat, that you're walking around nearly naked."

"I am. Long story." She moved across the room and sat down next to him on the mattress. "How are you feeling?"

"Pounding headache. Severe nausea. Stiff and aching joints and muscles."

She patted him on the back. "Good."

He glanced at her sideways. "That's good?"

"Yeah," she assured him. "You'll be feeling better in a day or so. Time enough for us to get supplies and get going."

He nodded. "Where's Darquiel?"

Kat motioned toward where Darquiel still lay still and unmoving.

Damian bolted to his feet. His legs were still shaky and unstable, and he fell in a heap beside Darquiel.

Kat reached out to him, but he swatted her hand away. "You've left her like this? She's starving to death. No one's even tried to help her." Bending over Darquiel's body, he touched her face.

Hades moved like a cat, quick and silent, across the room and loomed over Damian.

"Hades, don't hit him." Kat shook her head.

"She's had more help then she deserves," Hades said through clenched teeth.

Damian fixed his gaze on Kat. His eyes were dark and angry. "I'm surprised you didn't leave her out in the sun to bake. Compassion is not one of your stronger qualities."

Shaking with anger, Kat swallowed down the words forming in her mouth. She didn't need to take this crap from him.

He had no idea what she had done for him. What morals and ideals she had pushed aside to keep his love safe.

Hades grabbed Damian by the hair and lifted him to his feet. "You little bastard."

"Let him go, Hades." Kat shuffled next Hades and put a hand on his arm.

Hades tilted Damian's head so that he was looking into his face. "You know what she did for you? She fed that . . . that thing for you. Kat knew what kind of pain you would suffer if she had died. She did that for you, you dumb shit."

He let go of Damian and pushed away from him. Turning around, fists clenched at his sides, Hades marched over to his own bed.

Damian stood in front of Kat, swaying, staring at her. Tears welled in his murky eyes. "I'm sorry, Kat. I'm so sorry. I didn't mean what I said."

"Yes, you did. And it's all right. I *don't* have any compassion."

Damian wrapped his arms around her. He squeezed her to him and rubbed his hands up and down her back. "I love you, Kat."

Unsure of what to do, she patted him on the shoulder. She could feel his heart hammering in his chest while he sniffed at her hair and her neck. He kissed her softly below the ear. When she felt his cock stiffen, she tried to push him away.

Digging his fingers viciously into her sides, he held on. "I need you, Kat. Don't push me away."

"What's wrong with you, Damian?" She tried to distance herself. Her palms pressed into his chest but he clung to her like a leech.

He licked the side of her neck, trailing his tongue over her collarbone and to her shoulder.

"Damian, back off."

At the sound of Kat's angry voice, Hades swung around.

"I can't," Damian whined.

Kat stiffened as his teeth scraped her skin. When she realized what he was about to do, she grabbed his hair and pulled.

He bit down on her shoulder and pierced her skin. Pain, immediate and sharp, made Kat suck in a breath. At the same time, she tried to pry him off her, but his mouth remained attached to her flesh like a sucker on an octopus.

It took only a second for Hades to come to her aid, wrapping his beefy hand around Damian's neck and squeezing. Damian came off her shoulder with a definitive *pop*. Hades lifted him off the floor and punched him in the face. Damian's lips split open, blood spewing from his wounds and splattering across Darquiel's face on the cot behind them. Hades dropped him and Damian fell, unconscious, across her prone form.

Kat inspected her bloody shoulder. There were two puncture holes. "What the fuck is wrong with you!" she yelled at Damian, although he couldn't hear her.

"He's turning." Kat and Hades looked up toward the door of the longhouse. Nemo stood there, watching them with wide eyes and a knowing nod.

"Into what?" Hades asked.

"Into one of those." Nemo motioned to Darquiel. "A Dark Dweller."

"It's not possible," Kat argued, probing her wounds with her finger.

"I've seen it happen." Nemo came into the room and sat in one of the wooden chairs. "During one of the Dweller's raids, they badly injured one of our tribe and left him for dead. But he didn't die. And after a few days, it was apparent that he was changing."

Hades handed Kat a cloth to stem the bleeding. "How?" Hades asked.

"He was listless and incoherent during the waking hours, and during the night he was lively and . . . robust even. Some of the women of the tribe began to notice the changes in him, especially during the nightly hours. He was very alluring at night. Even I found myself drawn to him." Nemo turned his gaze from Hades and Kat and stared out the window. "Then one night we heard screams coming from his hut. What we found was more than most of us could stomach. He had ripped . . . young Brook's throat out and was . . . was feasting on her blood." He wiped a hand over his face and closed his eyes. "I cannot describe it any other way. He was completely covered with it and . . . smiling when we came upon him. He was even fully aroused."

Kat glanced at Damian, who still lay, passed out, on top of Darquiel. She wondered if he would have done the same to her if Hades had not pried him off. Cringing at the thought, she gently touched her shoulder.

"What happened to him?" Kat asked.

Nemo regarded Kat, his eyes filled with sorrow and regret. "I killed him and burned his body."

Hades nodded. "You are a great Chieftain, Nemo. You did what you had to do to protect your tribe."

"Yes, and now I have to make a decision once again for the sake of my people."

Kat noticed that he stared at Damian and Darquiel. Turning, she stood in front of him, blocking his view. "I can't let you kill them."

"He is changing. It won't be long before he loses control and ravages someone for blood."

"I'll take that chance."

"But I cannot."

Kat nodded. "I understand. We'll be leaving in the first light of day."

Nemo got up from his chair and walked over to Kat. He lifted up the cloth and inspected her wound. "They are both unconscious. It would be a mercy to end their lives now," he suggested to her softly.

"I can't. I need them to get to Van City."

He set the cloth back on her shoulder. "At any cost?"

She met his gaze and kept it. "Yes."

"You are a hard woman, Katarina. But I respect you none-theless."

"I'm not sure if that was a compliment."

Nemo moved away from her and toward the small table by the window. He picked up a clay pitcher of water and returned to where she stood.

"It was. Now remove that cloth and hold out your arm. We need to cleanse that wound."

Kat took off the dressing and held her arm out to the side. Nemo poured the water over her shoulder. It stung sharply while the liquid cascaded over her flesh. She bit down on her lip to stop from screaming.

"It's saltwater from our blessed ocean. It will hopefully heal you," Nemo assured her.

Hades watched on in interest. "How do you think they get like that, the Dark Dwellers?"

"I believe it is an infection or a virus." Nemo continued to stare into Kat's eyes as he answered Hades. "Passed on from one to the other."

Kat dropped her arm and took a distancing step in retreat. She understood his message, his warning. When Damian bit into her flesh, she had thought the same thing.

Hades glanced at her, concern furrowing his brow. "You can't be sure."

"No. I am not sure." Nemo also watched Kat.

Frowning, she turned away from their accusing stares. "Quit staring at me like I'm going to sprout fangs."

"Kat, it is a possibility."

She whirled around toward Hades. "You don't think I don't know that? The minute Damian put his mouth on me, the thought crossed my mind."

She collapsed on her bed and brought her knees up to her chest. Shivers vibrated up and down her spine. All of a sudden, she felt very cold.

Hades sat down next to her. "I'm sorry."

"Yeah, sure. Whatever. Doesn't really matter now, does it?"

"I am sorry, too, because now the request I ask of you will seem doubly difficult to bear." Nemo stood in front of them.

"What is it?" Hades asked

"As you already know, my wife was taken in the last raid. If you come across the Dwellers in your travels to the Vanquished City, I would ask that you seek her out, and if . . . if she can be saved, save her; if she cannot . . . then I wish for you to end her suffering."

Kat unfolded her legs and leaned forward, her elbows on her knees. "You want us to kill your wife?"

Nemo visibly bristled at her blunt words. "If it comes to that, yes."

"Listen, Nemo," Hades explained. "I understand how you feel, but we are not mercenaries. We are not going into Van to hunt down and kill these creatures."

"I'm not asking you to."

"Then what are you asking for?"

"A trade," Nemo offered. "All the supplies you can carry, for the chance . . . the slightest chance that you might run into these . . . people."

Hades glanced at Kat for approval. She shrugged. They needed the supplies, that was for sure. And if they did run into the

Dark Dwellers, she was certain she'd be shooting first, asking questions later.

"You have a deal, Nemo," Hades replied. "But know this, we don't know where these people dwell, and we will avoid all confrontations if we can so we can extract our treasure and be out of the city before anyone notices we were there."

"I understand," Nemo said solemnly. "I would not ask for more than what you have agreed to. I do not expect you to be heroes."

A low, hoarse cackling echoed in the room.

All eyes turned toward the sound. Darquiel sat up on the bed, cradling Damian in her arms, and licking his blood off her face.

"You won't have to search for the dwellers, they will find you," Darquiel revealed.

"They will find *you*, you mean?" Kat sputtered, her fists clenched with anger.

"Yes, Baruch can sense when I am near."

Hades turned to Kat and whispered. "This is too risky. We can bow out and make it back home. There will be other treasures."

"No," Kat, said rejecting his offer. "The Monolith is our ticket out of this shit. I won't let it go." She swore under her breath as soon as it was out of her mouth. Maybe he wouldn't notice that she included him as part of their team.

"Our? Like you and me, our?"

"No, yes, maybe . . . shit, it doesn't matter." She jumped off the bed. "I won't let it go. She knows where it is, and she'll lead us right to it. And if I have to fight off the devil himself, I will."

"It's not the devil outside you should worry about," Darquiel said, before she leaned down to Damian's slack mouth and touched her tongue to the blood.

Kat's stomach lurched. She was uncertain if the revulsion

was from watching Darquiel feed on Damian's blood or from the fact that she ached to join her.

Turning away from the grisly scene, she eyed Nemo. He had turned his back on them both. "Bring us our clothes and our weapons. It is time for us to go." Kat spoke the words, praying that Darquiel would lead them to the treasure and not to their deaths.

16

As the black sky started to lighten with the promise of the sun, Kat and Hades had their gear and supplies packed. Nemo proved true to his word and supplied them with food, drinking water, special sunblocking salve, and, surprisingly, motorized transportation.

The transport looked like a mini car, barely enough room for four people, with an umbrella covering it. Powered by the sun, it didn't move more than ten clicks an hour, but it would suit their purposes. Vanquished City was only about sixty clicks away, so they should make it by high noon. The sun would be too elevated and unyielding to run into any Dark Dwellers.

Or so Kat hoped.

Just as Hades brought Damian and Darquiel out from the longhouse, Kat strapped the last of the packs onto the rear of the transport. Both Darquiel and Damian were bound at the wrists.

Damian struggled under Hades's strong grip, but was too weak from the effects of the rising sun for his attempts to be anything but trivial. When he spied Kat waiting for them, he pulled harder at his restraints.

"Why did you let this asshole tie me up, Kat?"

Hades pushed both of them toward the cart. They stumbled, their legs unsteady.

"You're a danger, Damian," Kat said.

Damian swayed in front of her, defiantly staring into her eyes. "What? Are you afraid of me?" A small smile played at his lips.

Kat swallowed down the bile that rose in her throat. This was not the man she had spent three years with. He still looked the same—except that his pallor was paler and his eyes sunk in—but it was his manner and his demeanor that had so drastically changed.

She saw meanness in him. An almost twisted sadistic thrill of what he was changing into. He watched her not with adoration and respect, but with a kind of hunger. The way a cougar eyed an injured lamb, knowing that lunch would be soon served.

Not wanting him to see the dread that spread across her like a virus, Kat stood her ground. "No. I'm afraid of what I will do to you if you ever try to bite me again."

"You never complained before." He grinned.

It was not the playful boyish grin she was used to, but a wicked, malicious smile intended to hurt. Kat stared him down. She would not let him see that deep down inside a little razor-sharp knife stabbed at her heart.

Hades cuffed him on the side of the head. "Into the cart now."

Damian turned and glared at Hades, but did what he was told. He jumped up onto the cushioned seat beside Darquiel, who had already settled in without a word or a glimpse in their direction.

Hades gave Kat's hand a reassuring squeeze. She nodded briefly and then pulled her hand away. Accepting help from anyone proved difficult for her. She didn't need or want Hades's sympathy. Only trouble could be had, relying on other people's support. She didn't want thoughts and feelings to corrupt her thinking, especially since she was unsure if any of them would even make it out of Van City alive.

Kat turned toward Nemo, Leucothea, and the other Nerieds who had gathered to see them off. "Thank you for the supplies."

"You are most welcome." Nemo offered her his hand.

After a brief hesitation, she took it. He put his other hand overtop, holding her in a firm and comforting grip. "And thank you for what you will do."

"I haven't done anything yet. And don't count on me either. I'm not that reliable."

"But I know you will be true to your word. You are a stout and admirable woman, Katarina. Even if you do not think so." Nemo gave her a reassuring squeeze and then let go.

Kat nodded and was about to turn away when Leucothea rushed forward and wrapped her arms around Kat, hugging her tightly. Cautiously, Kat patted her on the back. She felt awkward as this slip of a girl pressed her bare breasts against her. She could feel the girl's heart pounding in her chest.

"Farewell, Katarina," Leucothea said. "I will miss you."

Unsure of what words to say, Kat just grunted.

Leucothea pulled back and smiled up at her. "I have something for you." Holding out her hand, Kat spied her leather eye patch lying in her palm. "I fixed it for you."

Kat took it and placed it over her eye, tying it up under her mass of ebony hair. She nodded at Leucothea and smiled fleetingly, uncomfortable with the obvious adoration the girl bestowed on her and the hard lump that formed in her throat. Rushing ahead, Kat jumped into the front seat of their transport.

Hades stepped up to Nemo and shook his hand. "Goodbye, Nemo. Thank you for everything."

"Farewell, Hades. I will pray to the gods that you travel swiftly and safely."

"Also," Hades said, "ask them to leave us some ammo for our guns. We're almost out, and I think we're going to need them."

Nemo smiled and nodded. "I will see what I can do."

Hades tipped his head and then jumped into the cart. He pushed the red button on the dash beside the steering wheel. The transport spurted to life. With a press on the metal pad, the cart accelerated forward.

Kat glanced back briefly as they left the sanctuary of the Nerieds' village. She had felt safe and comfortable for the first time in her life in their tiny community. Turning back around, she watched Hades as he drove the cart. He returned her look and smiled softly as if he knew what she was thinking. Uncomfortable, she averted her eyes and stared out across the approaching desert. That look was the reason why she never allowed anyone close. She could not allow anyone to see what was inside her mind. She had too many secrets, too many personal desires she would never allow anyone to see. Especially someone like Hades, who could easily subvert her thoughts and change them.

After several hours of travel they were right back in the middle of the arid wastelands. Except this time, they faired better. The canopy on the transport gave some relief from the heat, and the salve protected their skin from the harsh rays of the brutal sun. Even Darquiel and Damian did well out in the light, Hades thought, as he glanced over his shoulder at them.

They were slumped against each other in the rear seat. Both had their eyes closed, and their heads lolled limply on their necks. But it seemed like they were sleeping, and not unconscious, or dead.

Hades glanced at Kat. She rotated her wounded shoulder and winced, pain furrowing her brow. She had been silent during the trip, barely glimpsing his way. He thought he knew why.

"Is your shoulder buggin' you?"

"No."

"We should stop and clean it again with the ocean water Nemo gave us."

"Save the water. It's already too late."

Hades stopped the transport and turned to her. "We should still try."

Kat turned to him, her eyes frigid. "I feel a sharp stinging moving down my arm and across my chest. The virus is already in my body. There is nothing we can do."

She started to turn away, when Hades grabbed her wrist. He pulled her closer and leaned down to her mouth, pressing his lips to hers. The kiss was hesitant and unsure at first and then turned eager and hungry. When they broke apart, Hades kissed the tip of her nose, then her brow, finally resting his head against hers.

"I will not let you turn into one of them."

"I know. I expect you to do the right thing when the time comes."

Hades leaned back, keeping his hand cupped around her neck. Unable to speak, he looked her in the eyes and nodded. He sat back up and disengaged the brake. He pushed on the accelerator and propelled them forward, feeling just as barren as the ground they moved past.

He had consented to her request, but he was unsure if he could actually go through with it. The thought of killing Kat made his stomach turn and his heart ache.

"How far to the city, do you think?" Kat asked.

Hades stared ahead at the horizon, where dark, jagged peaks jutted toward the sky. Peaks he assumed could be nothing but city scrapers. "Thirty clicks till the limits, I think. Then another ten clicks in to ground zero."

Kat yawned. "Do you mind if I close my eyes for a while?"

"No, I'll wake you if there's any problem."

"Wake me in a bit so I can take over driving."

"It's all right. I've got it handled."

"I said wake me. . . ."

Hades laughed and put up his hand in defense. "Okay, okay. I'll wake you. Damnit, woman, you're stubborn."

Kat nodded curtly and then rotated in her seat to rest her head on the cushion, but not before Hades caught the lift of her mouth in a smile.

He could feel Kat pulling away from him. He had witnessed vulnerability in her, and she was now trying desperately to cover it up, hide it away, pretend it did not exist. As he clenched his hands he could still remember how her skin and hair felt under his touch. How her body had moved and writhed underneath his. How she moaned his name into his ear.

He hoped he would have that pleasure one more time before they met their end. With the city looming up ahead, Hades was certain this was the place where they would all succumb.

Dark. All encompassing. The smell of copper lingered in the thick, stagnant air.

A glaring spotlight flashed on. Kat couldn't shield her eyes as her hands were bound and she hung from thick iron chains bolted into the high ceiling. She blinked rapidly against the glaring light, trying to focus on her surroundings.

She glanced down at herself and saw that she was completely naked. She struggled against her restraints but it only swung her around. As she turned she noticed other bodies hanging from the roof. They formed a semicircle around her. Most chains held motionless forms with blood dried and congealed on their cooling flesh. Another chain held a woman. She was still awake and aware, even as blood dripped over her hairless form and down to pool underneath her webbed feet.

Kat stopped moving. Before her stood a man with long, dark hair and a disarming smile, complete with two long, pointed fangs protruding from his gums. He was ethereally beautiful. His face was sculpted with high cheeks and strong jaw. His black eyes glowed in the dark, like those of a cat or a wolf. He was dressed in a long, flowing robe and nothing else but a short clinging wrap that hung low on his hips and barely covered him.

His pale body was long and lithe. His muscles quivered as he moved closer to Kat.

"Katarina, my love."

Kat wanted to scream out, to curse him, but her voice froze in her throat. She opened her mouth but nothing came out.

He chuckled, and the deep throaty sound caressed her body. She cringed as her flesh betrayed her and quivered.

He moved even closer to her. She could feel his hot breath against her breasts as he spoke. Her nipples pebbled tightly, growing achy with want.

"This is a dream, remember? Anything and everything can happen. Even things you did not know you wanted."

He reached up and squeezed her breasts with his elongated, thin hands. His nails were long and they dug into her fleshy globes. Kat held her breath as the sharp pain turned to pleasure. He moved his hands over her, kneading her flesh and pinching her nipples between thumb and forefinger. He pulled and twisted them.

Kat opened her mouth to cry out, but no sound came.

He released her breasts and sighed. "You are more exquisite than Hades ever dreamed."

What did he mean, Hades's dream? Was Baruch invading his nightly images, too?

Kat wanted to move her legs. To kick out at him. But they would not move at her command. They hung uselessly beneath her.

He leered wolfishly as his eyes traveled lower to her sex. He leaned forward and pressed his mouth to her belly. He trailed his tongue over her flesh, intentionally scraping his fangs.

Kat sucked in a deep breath as he neared her sex. She could feel his teeth grazing over the sensitive skin just above her mound. He wanted her to know how easy it would be for him to sink them into her flesh. Even as shivers vibrated up and down her spine, her sex moistened with lust. She could feel the dew dribble down her thigh.

He also noticed. Running his finger over her thigh, he collected the cum onto his fingertip. He brought it up to his mouth and sucked it off.

"Delicious."

Kat closed her eyes as her cunt throbbed painfully. All she could imagine in her mind were his teeth scraping against her clit. Lolling it between his lips and sucking it into his mouth. Sucking on it fast and hard.

"Come, my servants, and grant me the feast I so desire."

Kat opened her eyes to see Damian and Darquiel step out of the dark and stand beside him. They grinned up at her as they each grabbed a leg and pulled her apart. Open and glistening for his eyes and mouth.

He licked his lips as he gazed down at her gaping cunt. He trailed one finger down her slit to her opening. He pushed his finger in and twirled it around, feeling every inch of her insides.

Kat's breath pushed out as ripples of intense pleasure swelled over her entire body. She almost orgasmed from his penetrating touches.

He slipped his finger out, brought it to his mouth, and licked it clean. He leaned forward and buried his face into her sex. He lapped at her slit. His tongue circled her clit. He sucked it into his mouth.

Kat tried to scream out as she came. But her moan did not resound.

She could feel cum gushing from her sex as sharp surges of pleasures washed over her and stole her breath.

He continued to lap at her as her juices flowed.

"Anyone else for a taste? I could feast all night on her."

Damian shook his head. "I've already had the pleasure."

Darquiel grinned. "I'd love a taste, Baruch."

Baruch moved aside and let Darquiel slide into his place at Kat's sex. She placed her thumbs on either side of Kat's inner lips and spread them even farther apart. She leaned forward and stuck her tongue into Kat.

Kat tried to kick and writhe away from Darquiel's invading tongue. But she could not, nor could she fight the extreme pleasure that crested over her. Another orgasm began to mount deep in her belly as she felt another set of fingers slide into her sopping wet cunt.

Darquiel lifted her head and gazed longingly up at Kat. Lust glistened on her lips.

"Oh, god, she tastes just like oranges."

"Kat!"

Kat startled awake as Hades shook her arm. She sat up and took in a gulping breath.

"Are you all right?"

She shook her head. "What?"

"Did you have a nightmare?"

Kat diverted her gaze. "No."

She could never tell him what she dreamed, what she felt while under the seduction of the Dark Dweller. One thing was certain, though; Baruch was intensely aware of her presence, and he definitely knew they were on their way into the city. Most likely was waiting for them.

"Did you want an orange?"

The offer raised her head and she stared at him to see if he was toying with her. She shook her head, knowing he couldn't possibly have been privy to her dream, and glanced out over the desert. The smell of her dream still penetrated her nose.

"I would love a piece."

Kat swung around and glared at Darquiel. She was sitting up in her seat, a knowing expression on her pale face.

Hades handed her a piece. She put it in her mouth and let her lashes flutter to her cheeks, savoring the juices. She opened her eyes and stared right at Kat. "I love that succulent flavor, don't you?"

Hades frowned at Darquiel's expression. "What's with you? You look almost happy."

"I had the most delicious dream . . . "

Kat was about to jump the seat and pound her fists into Darquiel's face, when Hades's gasp stilled her. "What the hell is that?"

Kat turned to where Hades pointed. In the blue sky, black churning clouds rolled across the horizon like a cattle stampede kicking up dust behind their stomping hooves. The clouds moved fast and fluidly, blacking out the sky like billowing smoke from a raging fire.

"Storm clouds," Kat stated, mesmerized by the rolling mass.

"Yeah, but what kind of storm?" Hades asked.

A gust of cold wind blew fiercely at them, causing the roof on the transport to rattle in fear.

"I was in a rainstorm once when I was a child. The wind blew up just like this," Kat recounted as she watched the progression of the clouds. It was almost on top of them.

"You know what? I remember that storm. But what I don't

remember is that sickly green color in the center of those clouds," Hades said.

Amidst the black and gray sweeps, an almost green luminance glowed from within. It wasn't a pretty leaf green, but the color Kat remembered from when her dog had once thrown up after eating too much grass. Kat's own gorge rose as she watched the clouds cover the sky above them.

The sun disappeared behind the cover and the temperature instantly dropped. The cold wind swirled around them, lifting Kat's hair in a dark dance around her face. She shivered as the chilling air surrounding her. "Damn, it's cold."

Hades shivered. "I never thought I'd see a cold day in this hell, but, damn, those clouds do not look inviting."

Kat studied the swirling mass of green and black, a feeling of apprehension creeping across her skin. "No, they certainly don't."

"We're almost at the limits. Hopefully, whatever is about to burst will hold off until we can reach that outcropping of buildings," Hades said.

Kat's eyes went to the horizon. Two small, crumbled piles of cement and rock loomed ahead. Doorways—openings into half-constructed concrete slabs and brick—were the only things left pronouncing them as buildings. But, still, a place where they could hold off the ever-increasing wind.

A long bolt of lightning cracked across the sky, startling everyone inside the transport. With a roar of thunder, the cart shook side to side, jerking Damian awake. "What the fuck was that?"

"Storm," Kat said.

"I thought it was God coming to strike me down."

Kat glanced over her shoulder at him. "I wouldn't count that out."

Rain erupted from the sky, pouring icy, piercing droplets onto the ground. Kat thought it felt like tiny steel balls hitting her skin in rapid succession. If the rain had fallen straight down, the roof on the transport would have protected them. Because the wind still blew, the sheets of rain pelted them as they drove forward to the safety of the destroyed buildings.

"Can this thing go any faster?" Damian complained. "I can walk faster than this."

Kat motioned with a nod. "Be my guest. But remember, lightning always strikes the tallest thing out there."

Damian jumped out of the cart. His head came about a foot above the roof. He ran alongside the transport and jumped back in. "I see your point."

"But won't we all die in this cart? It's the tallest thing out here;" Darquiel said.

"No," Hades explained. "I read somewhere that the rubber in the tires grounds the electricity from the lightning."

"Ah, right. Whatever that means," Damian said.

"It means, dumbass, that we all stay in the cart." Kat turned and glared at him.

"Fine by me, as long as I'm safe," Damian commented.

Another bolt of electricity cracked across the sky. Kat jumped as the thunder boomed overhead. She remembered the rainstorm of her childhood, but it was not nearly as violent as this. She recalled counting the seconds between lightning and thunder, determining the proximity of the storm like her mother had taught her. According to the tale, the storm was right on top of them and they could not outrun it.

Kat jerked as something hard hit the outside of her arm. She glanced down at her hand and noticed a coinsized red mark on her skin. Just as she was going to touch it, something else hit her arm. A small grayish-white rock hit her across the bicep and then landed on the floor of the cart. She bent down and picked it up, finding it cold and sticky in her hand. It was not a rock, but a round piece of ice.

She held it out for Hades to inspect. "This came from the sky."

"It's hail. We're driving right into a hailstorm."

With that, the clouds opened up and unleashed their ruin. In a violent barrage, small pellets of ice rained down on them.

Kat watched in shock as the storm raged around them. She knew that they would encounter various obstacles on their treasure hunt. Nothing in life was free. But to have the earth itself rage against them stunned Kat. She had faced many opponents in her lifetime, but nothing could prepare her for the onslaught of Mother Nature.

She was the toughest bitch Kat had ever come across.

17

Damian and Darquiel squeezed into the center of the back-seat, desperately trying to avoid the splattering of hailstones. The roof on the transport protected them from the sharpest torrent of hail, but some pellets still managed to bounce their way in and smack against their bodies.

"Holy shit, this is unreal!" Damian yelled over the roar of the falling hail as it battered the metal on the vehicle.

Kat watched in rapt fascination as the ice fell from the sky. She watched it rebound off the hard-packed earth and shatter into tiny frozen shards. They soon melted from the heat beneath the barren dirt. Everywhere she observed, little puddles formed and then evaporated. She had read about storms such as these. In the past, before the war, there were many types of weather. Now there were two: hot and cold. This seemed like a combination of both. A rare and unexpected occurrence.

She almost found herself smiling at its deliverance. Maybe the earth was changing again, this time bringing order back to the chaos.

Hades looked at her, worry furrowing his brow. "I think they're getting bigger."

"What?"

He held out his hand. A chunk of ice the size of a date rested in his palm.

"Shit."

"Yup, that's about it." He tossed the hailstone onto the ground. "We could be in a whole lot of trouble soon."

"What can we do?" Damian asked.

"Nothing. Except try to not get hit." Hades laughed.

"I'm glad you're having such a good time." Kat glowered at him.

"You know me, babe."

Kat shook her head. The man was incorrigible, but she couldn't help feel her lips twitch at his obvious glee.

A resounding clink sounded above them. Kat flinched and looked up. The metal roof had a sizable dimple in it. She watched in horror as three more dents appeared above. From the width and depth of the impression, Kat thought the stone had to be at least the size of a small orange.

"We're definitely in trouble."

Hades glanced up and then pulled the steering wheel sharply to the right. A solid ball of ice smashed into the front seat, right between him and Kat. Pieces of ice shattered onto their pants. He picked up a chunk and popped it into his mouth. He grinned and offered one to Kat.

She shook her head. "You have no idea what hazardous chemicals could be in that."

"Damn, girl, let loose a little. We're in a tiny cart with a flimsy piece of shit metal covering our heads, driving across barren wastelands no man can survive, with ice the size of base-balls falling from the black sky. Now, I don't think it can get any more absurd than this. So put this in your mouth and suck on it. We can't live forever anyway."

Kat smiled and shook her head. She took the offered piece, popped it in her mouth, and sucked on it.

"Kind of like a Popsicle. Ever had a Popsicle as a kid?"

"No—"

"Watch out!" Damian stuck out his hand between them, pointing to the front of the cart.

Hades tilted up his head just in time to swerve right around a head-sized chunk of ice that exploded onto the ground in front of them.

But he turned too sharp.

"Hang on!"

The cart began to tip. Kat grabbed on to the metal poles holding up the roof. She could feel herself slide down toward Hades, who desperately tried to keep the transport upright but failed with each moment. Finally it fell over onto its side. Kat's ass ended up positioned on top of Hades's shoulder, just hanging above his face.

She could feel his body shaking. Glancing down at him, she saw that he was laughing.

"Honey, if you wanted to sit on my face, you could've just asked."

Kat growled and kicked him in the ribs. He grunted but didn't stop laughing. Hail continued to fall, hitting Kat on top of the head. Fortunately these were only small-sized and not the enormous skull-basher that had caused them to flip.

"I'm glad you two are having fun. Could we fix this right now? Because I'm getting a headache from these ice rocks," Damian stated.

Kat glanced over at him. He had pieces of ice stuck in his hair, and rivulets of water running down his face.

"Are you hurt?"

He shook his head.

"How 'bout your friend?"

"I think my leg is broken. It went under the cart when we tipped," Darquiel murmured, barely audible over the clamor of the hail and wind.

Kat climbed out of the cart with Damian. Hades followed, a giddy smile still on his weathered face.

"Could you stop grinning like a fool and help us lift the cart?"

Hades grabbed hold of the cart and tilted it back onto its wheels. "Sorry, doll, I'm just having too much fun. You're quite the wild date, Hell Kat."

Kat glared at him but soon her mouth twitched and she couldn't stop the laughter that bubbled up from her gut. She doubled over, unable to contain the hysterics that erupted from inside. Her side began to ache from her shaking laughter, and tears ran down her face.

"What the fuck are you laughing at!" Damian demanded.

Kat opened her arms, tilted her face to the sky, and spun around. "This. This is fucking unbelievable!"

"You're fucking unbelievable." Damian pushed her hard. She stumbled backward and had to put out a hand to balance herself.

Hades made a move toward him. Kat grabbed him before he could punch Damian in the face.

"No. Let him be. You got something you want to say, Damian?" She walked up to stand right in front of him, almost touching. The tension rolled off him in waves. His teeth clenched and she imagined his muscles straining underneath his clothing.

They needed to have it out. Kat knew it, and she was sure Damian knew it, too. They had changed. Their dynamic had changed. It was time to set it straight.

"Here you are, having a good time, when Darquiel is hurt. Her leg is broken and you're out here dancing around like a fool."

"She'll live. Won't you?" Kat glanced over her shoulder at Darquiel. Hades had her up and sitting in the rear of the cart.

She nodded.

"You see?"

Damian tightened his mouth. "You can't be telling everyone what to do anymore. Things have changed. You're not the boss."

"Someone's got to keep everyone alive. Someone's got to lead. You gonna be leader, Damian? Who's gonna follow you? I'm certainly not, and I don't think Hades will either. Maybe Darquiel?" Kat suggested. "Yeah, how 'bout you go on your merry little way with your bloodsucking girlfriend and go into Van City and see how long you last? Not long, I guarantee you. You want to die, go right ahead, but don't take me with you. No matter what's happened, I still want to live." She leaned in closer to him, so only he could hear her next words. "No matter what runs in your veins, I would hope you still want to live. Because the Damian I knew and . . ." she paused, and then continued, "the Damian I knew would still want to live, to fight."

Damian smiled. "And what, Kat? And loved? Is that what you were going to say? 'The Damian I knew and loved?'" He smirked. "I didn't think you knew the meaning of the word."

"I don't. But you think this Darquiel does?"

Damian retreated and glanced over at the cart. "Yes."

"You're her food, dumbass. And now her pet."

He turned and glared at her with such venom, she had to take a distancing step back. "And that's what makes you so angry . . . that I'm not your pet anymore, and Hades will never heel to you."

He pushed past her and slid into the backseat of the cart next to Darquiel. He touched her briefly on the leg and left his bound hands there.

Kat wiped away the water that ran down her face. She stood there a moment more and let the hail pelt her cheeks and head. He had been right in some regard. She was angry that he had left her, that he had not the strength or fortitude to fight the hold Darquiel had forced on him. And about Hades. He had been right about him. The man would never bow down to her.

She turned back to the cart where they waited. Hades sat in the driver's seat and watched her, with no judgment in his eyes. No, he may never bow down to her but he would walk with her, at her side. Never in front, never behind. It was definitely something to think about.

"Let's get moving. We're wasting time." She slid into the seat and stared straight ahead.

Hades started the cart and they moved forward toward the buildings. As they neared, the hail stopped as if the doors to the heavens had slammed shut.

Kat leaned out of the cart and looked up at the swirling sky. "Now what?"

The sky was calm but for the sickly green clouds still churning menacingly above. Whatever it was, it was definitely not over.

"I don't like the feel of this," Hades commented as he steered toward the outcropping. "It's too calm. Something's brewing in those clouds and it isn't rain."

As they neared the destroyed buildings, Kat wasn't so sure that the crumbling concrete could protect them from anything. Miraculously, the doorway stood straight, with one wall still intact. There was a thick overhang of concrete that provided a small roof, but it didn't appear sturdy. Kat wasn't sure if they should trust it. They might be safer out in the open, depending on what came out of those dark clouds.

"Holy fuck!"

Kat swiveled toward Damian's voice. She squinted into the horizon, where he pointed. Her eyes must be playing tricks on her. What she saw could not be possible. She glanced over at Hades. His eyes were wide with shock, his lips pursed in worry.

"I have no clue what that is," Kat confessed.

"We're not in Kansas anymore."

Kat turned to regard Darquiel. Her eyes were wide; tears leaked from the sides.

"What the fuck does that mean?"

"It's from a story my dad read to me. It means we're all going to die," Darquiel muttered.

Kat turned to the front to gaze out at the wonder. The cloud layers looked like they had a hole in them and leaked out in one spot. The green, swirling mass formed a funnel shape; gradually its tip reached the ground.

Then it began to move.

The Earth shook beneath the vehicle. And it sounded like a roaring animal was charging toward them. The sound grew louder and louder. In the distance Kat watched in horror as dirt, debris, and leftover concrete swirled into the sky in the ever-increasing winds.

The funnel cloud moved across the ground in a quick and unpredictable path, laying devastation in its wake.

"Out of the cart!" Kat yelled over the increasing roar. "Run to the buildings!" She jumped out of the moving vehicle.

Hades stopped the cart and slipped out of the side, not far after her. He ran around the rear of the vehicle and unstrapped two packs from their supplies. He slung them over his shoulders and ran after Kat toward the outcropping.

"Wait!"

Kat and Hades both turned. Damian was helping Darquiel

out of the back, her leg bloodied and cradled against her other; she was clearly unable to walk on it.

"Carry her!" Kat yelled back.

"I can't. I'm not strong enough."

Kat could here the dejection in his voice. He had been strong once. Many times he had lifted her up and carried her. Usually to the bed or a wall where they could fuck. She had felt the power in his arms and in his legs. Now he must feel broken, like a neglected child's toy, by the weakening of his strength and his will.

She glanced at Hades. He shook his head but handed her the packs and ran back to the cart. He took Darquiel from Damian and, like a sack of potatoes, hefted her over his shoulder with little effort.

He glared at Damian. "You better run like a motherfucker. Because no one's going to stop to pick *you* up."

Damian nodded, but even from where Kat stood, she could feel the rage pour off him. He was like a pot of water heating on the stove with the lid on. Soon the boiling point would be reached, and the lid would pop off. She hoped they would not all get scalded.

"Hurry! It's coming!" Kat looked behind her as the green swirling mass edged closer. Rocks and debris pelted her in the body and face as the winds ripped around them. Soon the winds would be too powerful and would carry them off into the churning destruction. They needed to hold on to something or crawl underneath the ground.

They all ran as fast as they could against the pulling and pushing of the winds. The funnel was almost upon them. Kat could actually see large slabs of concrete twirling around in the clouds. They weren't going to make the buildings.

"We're not going to make it!" Hades yelled over the roaring din.

Kat searched for something, anything that might save them. She spotted a deep crevice in the ground that looked like the splitting of the earth's fragile skin.

"Into the ditch!" She pointed to the dugout.

They ran to it, feeling the incessant pull of the winds. Kat's cloak caught in a squall and flipped up around her. She could feel her feet lift.

Damian grabbed her hand and pulled her forward.

"Down! Down!" Hades screamed.

They all jumped into the ditch. Hades landed first, Darquiel half crushed beneath him. Kat went down with Damian on top of her, pressing her into the mud. She turned her head but still managed to swallow a mouthful of filthy rainwater. Afraid she might choke, she spat it out.

"No matter what happens, don't move. Don't get up," Damian whispered into her ear as he wrapped his arms around her.

Hearing the meaning behind his words, she wanted to turn and look at him. She wished things had turned out differently. His true self still lingered inside. She saw glimpses of it and heard it now in his voice.

"I'm sorry. I'm sorry for all that's happened. And all that's going to happen."

She heard the quiet desperation in his voice. Kat wanted to tell him it was okay. But it wasn't and never would be.

"I'm sorry, too," she said around the lump forming in her throat.

"We had a good run, though, didn't we?"

"Don't talk like it's over, Damian. I told you I would never give up, not until the last breath escapes my lips."

"I know. That's what I always loved about you, Hell Kat."

The sound of the roaring winds engulfed them as if a hundred motorcycle engines revved at once. Kat squeezed her eyes shut against the sound, trying futilely to block it from her ears.

She could smell the rain, the dirt, and the wet rocks as they swirled dangerously above them. The eye of the storm was upon them.

Glancing up, Kat grabbed on to a knotted root of a once grand tree poking out of the ditch. She gripped it, hoping somehow the branch would be strong enough to keep her from flying off into the ripping brutal winds.

"Hang on!" she yelled.

The ground seemed to shake around them as the screaming winds whipped over the ditch, raining dirt, rocks, and debris on top of them. She felt Damian move on top of her. To her horror, she felt his hands slip from around her body and his form lift from hers.

Still grasping the root in her hands, she cried out and tried to turn. She managed to turn over just as Damian was flipped into the air. Sitting up, she reached out with her hand. She caught his fingers and pulled back. While she held him suspended in the air, the winds viciously yanked on his legs.

Kat could feel her grip slipping. Her arm began to shake with strain. She didn't think she could hang on and still hold the tree root. Glancing behind her, she screamed for Hades. But her voice sounded muffled in the howling wind.

"Let go and save yourself!" Damian yelled. She could barely hear his words but knew what he said by the pain etched on his face and swimming in his wide eyes.

"No!" Her hand slipped, and she barely had him by two fingers.

"Let me go!"

Kat clenched her teeth and pulled with everything she had, but it was not enough. Damian's fingers slid from hers and he sailed into the swirling winds. She watched in horror as he spun high into the air and disappeared into the dark, swirling mass.

Kat squeezed her eyes shut and laid back into the ditch, clutching the tree root tightly in her trembling hands.

A warm palm cradled her cheek, and she knew that Hades had managed to turn and crawl to where she rested. Hot, bitter tears leaked out from the sides of her eyes and ran down her temples to drip into the cold, squelching mud. It brought her no relief from the icy shivers that racked her body.

She had lost Damian.

And just as fast as it came, the funnel moved on, turning erratically and back toward the city. The winds calmed and the roaring sound dissipated. Kat opened her eyes but did not move or relinquish the tight hold on the root.

Hades's face came into her view. "Are you hurt?"

She didn't answer. She felt numb.

"Are you hurt, Kat?"

Unable to form the words, she shook her head.

Hades pushed up and peeked out of the ditch. "The storm's gone. The clouds are breaking up." He glanced down at her again. "The cart's missing. Maybe we'll find it tossed by the wind."

"Yeah, and maybe we'll find Damian's torn body, too. Wouldn't that be great?"

Hades put an arm around Kat and helped her sit up. He stood and pulled her to her feet. Turning to Darquiel, he helped her up, too. She stood, wobbling on her bad leg.

"You might as well leave me. I will die without Damian."

Kat swung around, fists clenched, teeth gritted, and stared at her. "Good. I hope it's long and painful."

"You don't know the half of it," Darquiel smirked. "But you will."

Kat launched at her. She wrapped her hands around her throat and brought them down into the mud. She straddled Darquiel as she choked her.

"It's your fault this happened. If Damian had still been human, he would have had the strength to fight. He would have held on to me."

Darquiel brought up her hands and raked her nails across Kat's face. Three deep scratches lined each cheek. Kat let go of her throat, brought her hand back, and punched Darquiel in the face. Repeatedly, she struck Darquiel until her face was a mess of blood.

Hades grabbed her fist as she raised it for her next punch. "Enough." He yanked her off Darquiel.

Kat turned away from the girl. Rage encompassed her whole body. She could think of nothing but killing Darquiel. She thought that feeling the life leave her soulless body would replace the deep ache of Damian's loss.

"Damian is gone because of your selfish wishes," Darquiel accused.

Kat turned around and glared at Darquiel as she pushed herself into a sitting position.

"You brought us here to this wasteland. It was your selfish quests that made him weak." Blood bubbled at Darquiel's mouth. "He was broken long before I met him."

Kat scrambled out of the ditch and walked quickly across the drying dirt to get away. If she could, she would run, but her legs ached. She had fallen on them awkwardly. She didn't want Darquiel's words to seep into her mind. She didn't want to hear the accusations in her tone and know that all Darquiel said was true.

"Kat!" Hades called.

Kat didn't peer back, but kept her head straight ahead and walked.

"Kat!" His voice got closer. He grabbed her arm and stopped her strides. "What are you doing?"

"Nothing. Leave me be."

He grabbed her by the upper arms and shook her. "You can't run away."

"I'm not."

"It's not your fault."

"He died because of me. Because I made him come here."

"He died because the wind whipped him away." Hades motioned to the sky. "He died because this world is fucked up and unsafe."

Tears welled in her eyes. Hot, gushing tears. Tears of rage and sorrow.

Hades gathered her close in his arms, pressing her into the warmth and safety of his massive body. Pressing his lips to the top of her head, he murmured, "He died because there is no certainty of this life. We will go when we go. Nothing can change that. We can fight as long as we can, but in the end, we will all die. You couldn't have changed that for him."

Kat closed her eyes against the assault of emotion that ravaged through her. She wrapped her arms around Hades and cried. She sobbed and wailed. Never before had she let go. All the anger, sorrow, and rage she had ever felt poured out of her in hot, stinging tears and grievous moans. She emptied all the pain, suffering, and wrongdoing she had ever committed or suffered onto Hades.

She didn't feel it when he picked her up and brought her down to the ground to cradle her in his lap, and she didn't hear the soft words of sympathy whispered into her ear. She only felt years of pent-up frustration and anger leak from her soul. It poured down her face and dripped onto the barren land where it quickly evaporated as if it never existed.

18

Kat didn't know how long she sat cradled in Hades's arms, but by the looks of the clear blue sky, it had been a long while. There was not a single cloud left when she glanced up.

She studied Hades and sighed with relief to see no sympathy in his face. That was the last thing she wanted, especially from him. She rubbed at her eyes, wiping away the last of the stored-up tears. They felt puffy and raw. After that long of a crying jag, she could just imagine the state she was in.

Kat dropped her gaze and untangled herself from his arms. She stood and surveyed the wasteland. Everything was seemingly still and quiet as if nothing had happened. As if no life-ripping storm had charged through.

"Where's the vamp?" she inquired.

Hades stood and flexed his legs. She imagined they were very sore and cramped from sitting for so long.

"She's in the building. To get out of the sun."

Nodding, Kat glimpsed at the sky. It was getting warm again. Sweat trickled down her neck and into her shirt.

"We should, too. There's water in the packs I saved." He raised the two bags he had taken from the cart.

She nodded again, relieved that the man was reliable and thinking ahead. She needed his level head to straighten out hers. She started to walk toward the crumbled outcropping.

"Kat?"

She turned back to him.

His brow furrowed with worry. "I . . ."

"Don't." She put her hand up to stop any more words. "It's over. It never happened. And I never want to be reminded of it . . . ever."

"Hey, I was just going to ask if you could rub my ass because it's killing me." He massaged his hands over his butt and smiled.

Kat chuckled. Damn if the man was good for her.

"I'll rub yours if you rub mine." He moved up next to her.

"Maybe later."

Smiling, he traced a finger over her lips. "I'll hold you to that."

She nodded and continued to walk toward the burned-out building, Hades matching her stride for stride.

They walked through the still standing doorway into fallen concrete and decades of dirt and debris. Darquiel huddled in the corner under an unstable shelf of concrete that jutted out obscenely from what would have been the second floor. She had overturned a concrete block and used it as a chair. Opening her eyes as they neared her, she said nothing.

Kat hunkered down against the only complete wall standing in the shade. Hades handed her a canteen and she drank lustily. She felt dehydrated from her crying. Who knew there could be so much water in one body? She handed it back to Hades, who took a greedy gulp.

He motioned to Darquiel. "Do you need some water?"

She nodded and took the offered canteen.

Kat watched the girl and noticed that the bruises and cuts she had inflicted on her were already healing. The wounds to her lips and cheek had scabbed over. And the bruising under her eyes was yellowing.

Kat raised a hand to her own face. The deep scratches Darquiel had given her were sore and still tacky with blood. Kat wiped the residue on her shirt.

"You'll start to heal faster in time," Darquiel commented.

Kat glanced up at her. "Is that right?" she said sarcastically, grabbing the canteen from her. She didn't want to hear anything the girl had to say, especially about what Kat might possibly be turning into. After rubbing the top of the canteen with the hem of her shirt, Kat took another long swig.

"And you'll soon find you have a thirst that no amount of water can quench," Darquiel remarked.

Avoiding the girl's intense gaze and uncomfortable comments, Kat capped the canteen and returned it to Hades. She wiped her mouth with the back of her hand. Her lips still felt dry and cracked, and her throat raw and sore. It was from the crying and nothing more.

"How long till nightfall?" she asked Hades.

"Three or four more hours."

"Can we make it to the center?"

He shook his head. "I wouldn't want to, either. Ground zero is the last place I want to be when it gets dark." He glanced briefly at Darquiel.

"He's right. Full dark is hunting time," Darquiel agreed.

Kat stood and moved close to Hades. She turned them away from Darquiel's sight and spoke lowly. "We don't need her anymore. We're here at the city limits. It's just a matter of time that we find what we're looking for."

"It would be easier with her. She knows exactly where to go."

"I don't trust her. Even more now that there's nothing holding her here."

"I don't either," Hades agreed. "But I think she's more useful with us than left to her own devices. If this Baruch can feel her, she can feel him. She will be able to tell us when he is near. Like an early warning system."

Kat rubbed a hand over her dry mouth again. "Yeah, but will she? She could be leading us right to them."

"Hey, I'd rather face them head-on anyway. I hate all this sneaking-around bullshit." He grinned and put his arm around her shoulders, squeezing her close. "We got to go some time, right, babe? Why not take out as many of these fuckers as we can while we're at it?"

Kat couldn't argue with his logic. It made perfect sense. To a crazy ass-bitch like her anyway.

"Agreed." She turned around and grabbed one of the packs. "We should keep going until we can find a safe place to hole up." She glanced up at the slanted concrete roof. "I don't trust this one."

Hades picked up the other pack. "Let's do it." He gestured to Darquiel. "Can you walk?"

After a brief nod, Darquiel stood and followed them out of the destroyed building in search of something else sturdy enough to hide them from the things that went bump in the night that only she knew of.

While the sun slipped down into the west, they found a building intact. All four walls and roof were still standing, erect and proud. The glass had been incinerated, of course, but it would provide the shelter they required. With open space all around the area, they could see what moved in every direction.

The building had been gutted inside except for a few broken shelving units and a dirt-encrusted counter that lined one wall. Kat unearthed a sign just outside the main door. It was big and bulky, but she could only make out the number seven. Fire and age had blackened everything else. Must have been some place important if they had built it so strong. It was the only building standing for clicks.

Hades moved around some shelves and broke off planks so they didn't have to lie on the dirt floor. He arranged them in a triangle. In the middle, he put the little hot plate Nemo had supplied them. It would give off enough heat without light for them to sleep comfortably and safely.

As the sky darkened and the air around them chilled, they sat in their little triangle and ate dried meat and fruit. Kat consumed more than her share. She felt ravenous. After her fill, her stomach still growled. She hoped the others didn't hear. But as Darquiel smiled slyly at her, she knew the vamp knew exactly what was going on inside her.

"I'll take first watch," Kat stated as she stood up.

"No, you need the sleep," Hades protested.

She cocked her shotgun and glared down at him. "Don't tell me what I need."

"Right. No problem."

"I'll do a perimeter sweep in a clockwise rotation every twenty minutes. My primary position will be at the main doorway."

Hades pushed to his feet and saluted her. "Roger, chief."

She rolled her eyes and turned to march away. Hades grabbed her arm and swung her around. "Be careful."

"Yeah, yeah." Kat felt her stomach tighten and her heart flutter as he leaned down to her mouth. He pressed a soft kiss to her lips. Her knees weakened and her thighs turned to liquid. The man had powerful hormonal stimulators.

She wanted nothing more to do but move into the warmth and security of his arms and let him take her. She remembered clearly their time in the trees of the Neried village. She could still feel his hands on her flesh and taste the musk of his skin. It was the first and only time she had ever let go and surrendered completely to someone. It was liberating and binding all at the same time.

She stared into his eyes and smiled softly as he pulled back. He winked at her and grinned. The man was a charmer. She shook her head and turned to go to her post at the main doors.

Hades watched until she was just a shadowy form outlined at the entrance to the building. He was worried about her. The change was upon her. She was fighting it, but he could still see it happen. She ate like a starved dog and still she hungered. And her thirst was unquenchable. He even noticed that the scratches on her cheeks had scabbed over. Soon they would begin to fade just like the vanishing cuts on Darquiel's face.

He also worried about her mental state. Damian's loss had triggered a trap door in her soul. He had felt it pour out of her as he held her tightly in his arms. He had never experienced such heart-wrenching emotion before. He couldn't believe she had been holding all that in for so long. She prided herself on being so tough and jaded, but he knew it had cost her far more than she wanted to admit.

As he had paid his fair share, he knew the costs of this life. But one thing was certain to him now if they survived this job: He promised himself that he would take Kat away. With the money they got from the treasure, he would buy two bikes, pack it up with as much food and supplies as they would need, and he would take her up north. To God's Country to start over.

That's what they called it. A land where the water was un-contaminated and the air cool and breathable. Where land was available to purchase and build upon. It would be their little utopia. A place where they could be free. And maybe even raise a family.

That last thought had him chuckling. Kids. He could just

imagine how they would turn out with him and Kat as parents. He didn't think the world was ready for that, quite yet.

Hades turned and sat on one of the planks in the triangle. Darquiel was lying on her side with her legs pulled up to her chest. Her eyes were closed, but he could tell she was not asleep.

"She's changing." Her voice was low, as not to be heard beyond their triangle.

"I know."

"For what it's worth, I'm sorry." She opened her eyes.

"You should tell Kat that."

"She won't listen to me. You know that."

"Yeah. Can't blame her, though."

After a pause, Darquiel muttered, "No, me neither."

Hades watched her as she turned onto her back and stretched out her legs. He couldn't quite figure her out. She was like two people inside. A scared little girl and a cunning seductive woman. He supposed it was because she had been that scared little girl when she was taken and turned into this . . . this abomination.

"How long does it take, the change?" Hades asked.

"A few days usually if you don't fight it or have the capacity to fight it." She turned her head to look at him. "In Kat's case, I give her another couple of days before it really gets bad."

"Give me an idea of what's 'bad.'"

"Vomiting after eating. Feeling weak and listless. Uncontrollable rages at night. Soon she'll start viewing you as food. She won't want to, but she won't be able to fight it."

"There has to be a way to control it. You did eventually."

"That was over a long period of time, Hades. I went through weeks of terrible pain and suffering until I succumbed to my hunger and fed. After I fed regularly, it was easier to control. I could go days without blood, weeks even." She sat up on her plank. "The only other thing that might control it is sex."

"Sex?"

"Yeah, fulfilling one lust for another. At least from what I've seen, sex is an integral part of the Dweller system," Darquiel explained.

"Why?"

"Well, needing to feed is like being on the edge of orgasm but never ever going over. It's like being on the pivotal point of sneezing but never doing it. When you feed, it is like a powerful climax. Sex would sate the hunger for a while. Until the buildup becomes too overwhelming—then only blood can satisfy it."

Hades nodded. It made some sense. And gave him some ideas on how to fight Kat's own change. She might not be receptive to it, but he would suggest it anyway.

"But it gets hard. Especially so close to *him*."

Hades saw her shiver, and he could hear the fear in her voice. "Can you feel him?"

She turned her gazed down to the ground. "Yes."

"Is he close?"

She shook her head. "No . . . not yet."

"You'll tell us when he comes?"

She raised her head and gazed vacantly at Hades. "Yes, I'll have no choice."

Nodding, Hades lay back on the board. He would get some sleep knowing the enemy was not quite upon them. There was no doubt in his mind that he would need all his strength and all his wits soon enough.

Baruch's mocking laughter still rang hauntingly in his head like a deadly warning.

19

_____

Leaning against the doorway, Kat peered out into the dark. The moon was out and gave some light to the black surroundings. She could see dark shapes she knew to be concrete slabs and rocks. Nothing moved. There was not even foliage to rustle.

She had done four perimeter sweeps. All was still and quiet in every direction. The only things she could hear were Hades's soft snores. Although he seemed larger than life, he was still just a man. With dreams, fears, and silly little nuisances, like snoring, that endeared him to her.

Damn, she was getting soft! She had to snap out of it if she wanted to keep her edge. The edge that had kept her alive for this long. Without it, she feared she would be just like everyone else—a lamb fit for the slaughter. She had to stop thinking about Hades in that way, like a hero, or her rescuer, or food.

Kat blinked. *Food?* Now, where had that come from? Her stomach rumbled again and she rubbed a hand over it. She could feel it contract painfully with hunger. Having eaten only hours ago, she could not be hungry again.

But you are hungry....

Kat shook her head and braced herself against the doorway. Dizziness engulfed her and her head ached as if it were being crushed in a powerful vice.

You are hungry ... but not for dried fruit and meat. You want something warm and alive. Something thick and tangy. The one thing that pumps in us all ... blood!

"No," she whispered. "No. I won't do it."

"Do what, love?"

Kat turned toward the silky voice. She was no longer in the burned-out building but in the cold, dank, dark room of her nightmares.

Baruch stood before her, smiling, wearing only his long, dark, flowing robe. He was naked underneath and she could clearly see his cock. It was erect and pointed straight at her in accusation. She felt a sudden tightness in her cunt as she gazed upon his splendor.

"I won't succumb. I won't be like you," she said breathlessly.

Baruch's grin widened, displaying long, sharp fangs. "I don't want you to succumb, Katarina. I want you to surrender. But I want it willingly. Because it would be that much sweeter coming from you."

"Fuck you."

He laughed. The sound reverberated around the cement room and vibrated over her skin, coaxing pleasant shivers from her body. "In time. But first you must eat." He stepped aside and swept his arm to the side.

Behind him was a long stone altar. Someone was strapped onto its surface. Unnervingly curious, Kat stepped forward. She closed her eyes in pleasure as a sweet scent wafted to her nose. She breathed it in and felt euphoric and lusty.

Approaching the altar, her gaze traveled over the stone slab. Hades was strapped down; blood trickled from several wounds over his naked body. His mouth was stuffed with some sort of fabric; he gazed up at her, imploring with his eyes. Long, deep cuts marred his beautiful form. Over his chest, arms, legs— and his neck; the blood flowed the fastest there.

Baruch stepped up next to her and placed his hand on her shoulder, massaging it tenderly. "He is for you, Katarina. I know you want him. I can see it in your face, feel it in the trembles of your body. Here he is, the great Hades bowed down before you." Baruch ran his hand up and down her back. "I know that's how you like them."

Kat wanted to turn away, return to the burned-out building where Hades was sound asleep snoring. But she couldn't. The hunger deep in her gut would not allow her to. She had never felt such power before. It was unstoppable.

She brought her hands up to touch Hades. He flinched as she settled them over his chest. She could feel his heart race under her palm. Power surged through her, knowing that his heart raced because of her. She rubbed her hands over his muscles, over the bleeding cuts. Soon her hands were crimson with his blood.

She moved them down over his stomach and down to his cock. Touching him gently, she could feel him twitch under her caresses.

Baruch moved behind her. She could feel his erection pressing against her ass. Giving him room to maneuver, she bent a little forward. She didn't care. She wanted him there. Wanted to feel him inside her. She wanted it more than she had ever wanted anything before.

Baruch brought his hands around her waist and slowly unzipped her pants. He pushed them down past her ass to her knees. She could feel him rub his cock against the separation of her ass cheeks. When he easily slid into her wet cunt, she moaned encouragement.

She bent over Hades. He looked up at her, pain and betrayal swimming in his eyes. Unnerved by his gaze, Kat turned her attentions to his cock. She still caressed him with her red-splattered hands. She couldn't help herself.

As Baruch slid in and out of her, he pressed on her back, pushing her forward. Her face hovered over Hades's blood-slicked skin. She turned her head, trying to divert the intoxicating smell that enveloped her. His blood smelled like fresh-churned honey.

Kat let out a gasp as Baruch pumped into her hard and fast. He kept pressing down on her. Pushing her down. Pushing her into Hades's blood.

"No," she protested.

"Yes, my love. It is what you want. Just as you wanted my cock in your cunt, you want to taste his blood."

Kat shook her head. "No."

"Taste him. Take him! You are more powerful than him!"

She pushed away from the altar and into Baruch's arms. He wrapped himself around her possessively. His hand cupped her breasts through her shirt as he continued to move his cock in her.

"You are a foolish woman, Katarina," he whispered seductively in her ear. "Now I will fuck you raw while you watch him die."

Two Dwellers stepped out of the shadows. Damian and Darquiel smiled at her as they advanced on the altar. Talons poked obscenely from their fingers. They raised their hands in the air over Hades. They brought them down in a vicious arc. . . .

"No!" Kat pushed away from Baruch and reached out toward Hades.

"Kat!"

Kat shook her head and looked around. She was in a heap on the dirt ground. Cold sweat slicked her skin. She was back in the burned-out building.

It had been a dream. A terrible, vulgar nightmare that came extremely close to seducing her.

"Kat! We got company coming!"

Scrambling to her feet, she ran to where Hades's voice came from. He was standing over Darquiel as she twisted and turned in her sleep. She was mumbling.

"What's wrong?"

Hades pointed to Darquiel. Darquiel's eyes flashed open. "He's coming. He's coming."

"Shit."

"Yup, and then some." Hades bent down and retrieved his shotgun from the ground. He chambered a round.

"I'll sweep north, you sweep south. Anything that moves, shoot it," Kat ordered.

"We don't have much ammo. I don't want to waste it."

Kat patted the knives strapped to his legs. "I don't think these will be much use if they get in close."

"Yeah, probably not, but I'll bleed any fucker that gets near me."

She smiled. Then it faded as she remembered too clearly her waking dream. She grabbed onto his arm and pulled him down. She wrapped a hand around his neck and pulled him to her mouth. She kissed him feverishly, passionately. He moaned into her and wrapped a hand in her hair. Breaking from the kiss, she rested her forehead on his.

"Don't let them take you," Kat pleaded.

"I won't."

"I mean it. Save a round. No matter what, don't let them take you."

He cupped her face in his hands and pressed his lips to hers again. "I won't."

She nodded and ran to the front of the building. She hunkered down into a shooter crouch and peered into the night.

Nothing moved. She searched the area slowly. She could see nothing but rocks and forgotten remnants of a long-ago society.

Yet something stirred behind her.

Turning quickly, she shouldered her gun and then lowered it when she saw who it was. "Damnit, Hades."

"Sorry, I don't think we should separate."

He set Darquiel down on the ground. Her eyes still wide and frightened, she slumped over like a rag doll. He squatted down next to Kat, turning in the opposite direction.

"Are you scared?" Kat chided.

He nodded, smiling. "Yeah, a little."

She stared back into the darkness. "Me, too."

They continued to watch the night. But nothing moved and they heard no sounds except Darquiel's incessant mumbles.

"Are you sure she's right?" Kat asked.

"I don't know. She looks frightened enough."

Kat crouched near Darquiel and poked her in the arm to get her attention. Darquiel moved her head toward Kat, but seemed to stare right through her.

"Are you sure he's coming? I don't see anything. You didn't forget to tell us they were invisible or anything, did you?"

Darquiel suddenly sat up straight and stiff like a wooden board. "He's here."

Kat jumped up and spun around, her gun aimed. "Where?"

Hades also scrambled up and searched the area, gun pointed. Kat peered into the dark, but saw nothing. No shadows. No anything.

"He's here. He's here. He's here!" Darquiel's voice rose with each word until she was screaming.

Kat spun around in confusion. She pushed up against Hades. They stood back to back and swept their weapons back and forth.

"I can't see anything," Kat whispered.

"Me neither."

"Can you shut her up?"

Darquiel continued to mewl the same words over and over, but she was now standing, her arms wrapped around herself in a protective hug.

Another sound vibrated over top of Darquiel's chanting. A loud, reverberating, thumping sound. Like an amplified swoop of a bird's wing.

Kat veered her shotgun toward Darquiel. "Hey, shut up!"

"What's that noise?" Hades swung around, searching the area.

"I don't know. It's getting closer."

Darquiel stopped cold, turned toward Kat, and grinned. The way the moonlight played across her pale skin made her look like an animated skeleton. "He's come for you, Katarina."

Suddenly they were there.

Standing behind them. Four of them. Kat and Hades swung around, but it was too late. They didn't even get a shot off before the intruders yanked their weapons viciously from their hands.

Baruch stepped out of the shadows and into a beam of moonlight. He was smiling as if greeting longtime friends. "How lovely to finally meet. I've been having such wonderful dreams about you both."

Kat unsheathed her knives. She twirled them in her hands, ready to strike out. "Fuck you, bloodsucker."

"As I told you before, love, you will have that pleasure soon enough."

Kat let out a battle yell and rushed at the nearest Dweller. He sidestepped her with such speed, she didn't see it happen. His hand came back and hit her across the face. The powerful blow forced her to stumble sideways. She glanced behind her as Hades attacked another one.

He, too, missed and was hit across the head. He staggered and fell to his knees. The Dweller loomed over him and kicked him in the ribs. Hades lifted off the ground and landed on his side, his arms cradled to his stomach. Both his knives dropped from his hands.

Kat turned around shakily. Her knees were still wobbly. She spun her knives around again and made another rush. This time she faked to the left and went right, so that when the Dweller sidestepped he stepped, into her knife. She plunged it deep into his gut. She pushed and twisted, finishing the job.

He grabbed her by the throat and squeezed, lifting her off the ground. Soon black spots popped up before her eyes. The world seemed to be spinning. As if her limbs were leaden, she dropped her hand from the knife still stuck in the assailant and closed her eyes. She had lost the struggle. But before everything went black, she heard Baruch.

He was laughing. Joyous, cheerful laughter. And she almost felt like joining in.

20

When Kat opened her eyes, she wasn't sure if she was back in one of her dreams or if what she witnessed was real.

She found herself on a bed. A big opulent one, with a canopy and sheer red drapery hanging from it, enclosing her in a frothy crimson cloud. The aroma of fresh bread and something sweet and tangy floated on the stale air to her nose. Her stomach rumbled in response to the delectable smells. Lifting her head, she peered through the curtains, trying to determine where she was and if she was alone.

The room was large, furnished with fancy dressers, tables, and a long sofa covered with pillows. The bed had the same type of pillows in deep, rich colors. Kat picked up one and squeezed it. The fabric was soft and smooth against her palm. A material she'd never felt before. Putting it to her face, she rubbed it over her cheek, enjoying the way it felt on her skin. A familiar scent permeated the fabric. She tossed the pillow onto the bed.

Baruch. This had to be his room.

Glancing down at herself, she searched for her weapons.

Naturally, they had been confiscated. *A girl could hope*, Kat thought. She pulled aside the curtain and slid off the bed. Peering around the room, it appeared to her that she was, thankfully, alone. For now anyway. Two platters of food were set on the low wood table in front of the black sofa. Her stomach growled again, clenching painfully. There was no ignoring it. She had to eat.

When she reached the table, Kat eyed the food piled on the plastic plates. There were some pieces of sliced apple, and vegetables like cauliflower and tomatoes. Everything appeared fresh. Again, her stomach cramped and she doubled over. Reaching out, Kat grabbed a handful of food and shoved it into her mouth. As she chewed, bits and pieces fell from between her lips. She couldn't eat it fast enough.

While she ate, she glanced around the room, taking in the lavish surroundings. Some of things scattered around the room appeared foreign to her. Luxuries of an overindulgent and decadent past, she assumed, excavated from around the city. Tall, elegant glasses with long, thin stems stood next to an equally elegant glass decanter on the polished table. Both filled with a red liquid. Kat didn't even want to consider the source of the crimson substance.

"Are you thirsty?"

Kat whipped around to stare at the bed she had previously occupied. Behind the red gauze, Baruch and two women lounged on the soft cushions.

How did they get there? She was certain there had been no one else in the room. Peering past the headboard, Kat noticed a crack in the wall. A door, possibly?

Baruch swept aside the curtains and stood. He wore the same black robe she remembered from her dreams. Thankfully, he wore something else under it, a pair of shiny black pants that flowed like water when he walked toward her. His chest was bare, and she couldn't help but notice the way his muscles rippled while he moved.

Averting her gaze as he neared, Kat tried to concentrate on the anger about the attack and capture. But as his tantalizing smell reached her nostrils, making her knees weak, she could hardly think at all.

He picked up the container from the table. "Would you like me to pour you a glass?"

Kat took a few distancing steps back. The little hairs on her arms were standing to attention, and it felt like fingers were playing up and down her spine. His presence unnerved her in ways she didn't want to consider.

"No," she grunted.

Chuckling, he poured the red liquid into two of the elegant glasses. He picked his up and took a sip, studying her over the rim.

"I'm pleased to finally meet you, Katarina. In the flesh, so to speak," he drawled as his gaze panned the length of her.

She shivered from the way he scrutinized her as if he was trying to decide how much of her he could fit on his plate.

"That makes one of us."

As he took a step toward her, Kat peered around the room, searching for a weapon. Anything to keep him at bay. She didn't think she could handle it if he touched her. And not because he repulsed her—no, it was because he didn't.

She reasoned that it was the virus inside her that reacted to him. There could be no other logical thought for the way her body flared in response to his presence, or for the erotic images that flashed behind her eyes when she looked at him.

With a sly grin, he took another step toward her. "I can see in your eyes that you question why you are here. That you mistrust the feelings racing through your body."

Taking another step back, Kat ended up pressed up against

the concrete wall. Stupid mistake. She hadn't been concentrating on where she was going. Now she was trapped.

Baruch took one last step, closing the already small gap between them. "Don't be afraid, Katarina."

She smirked, "Listen, jerk-off, I don't know the meaning of fear."

He chuckled and tilted his head, appearing to study her like a lab animal. "You amuse me."

"Fuck you," she growled with a sneer. Lifting her arm, she swiped at his wineglass and pushed at him so she could run past. The glass fell from his hand to shatter into tiny pieces on the floor.

But Baruch never flinched. The force of her shove did nothing to push him away. Instead, he shackled one wrist and pushed her up against the wall, her arm raised above her head. He was strong. Stronger than any normal man; her struggles went unnoticed.

Leaning forward, he brought his face a few inches from hers. She could smell the sweet wine on his hot breath as he nuzzled his nose against her cheek.

"Fighting me is pointless, Katarina." Flicking his tongue, he lathed the lobe of her ear. Shivers rushed down her spine like cascading water. He pitched his voice low. "We are connected, and no amount of denial and refusal will change that. Ever."

Turning her head to the side, Kat tried to pull away from his mouth and the delectable things he was doing to her ear and neck. But she had nowhere to go. He had her pinned with his arms and his body. She could feel his heat flowing from him through the cotton of her shirt. Her nipples grew into hard, tight peaks in response. Sweat trickled down her back past the waistband of her pants to pool between the cheeks of her ass. His proximity was making her hot and sweaty, as if a small fire had erupted inside her body, flames licking at her insides.

Cursing to herself, she tried to push down her growing desire. The last person she wanted to lust after was the vile man in front of her. Although he looked sexy and dangerous, her usual criteria for a man, she knew him to be cruel and heartless beneath his delicious exterior. Despite the fact that she knew these things, believed these things in her heart, her body craved him. A throb, deeply rooted and intense, mounted in her sex, solidifying her body's ultimate betrayal.

He chuckled and licked the side of her neck. "Mmm, I see my attentions are not going unrewarded." He whispered into her ear, "I can smell your desire dripping between your legs."

Between clenched teeth, she snarled, "The only thing I desire is your head on a stake."

Laughing again, Baruch nibbled his way along her jawline. Closing her eyes against the surge of pleasure washing over her as he nipped at her flesh, Kat brought her other hand up to his bare chest and tried to push him away. Her efforts proved futile. It was like pushing granite. And his skin felt so deliciously warm under her palm.

Clenching her hand against the need to stroke it over his smooth, muscular chest, Kat tried to rein in her lust. She didn't want this with him. He was the enemy. Sex with Baruch would be disastrous. To her and to everything she had gone through to get here. Everything she had experienced with Hades. Succumbing to this raging hunger racing through her body would belittle everything she had come to feel for Hades. She wouldn't do that to him. She found she cared too much.

With all the strength she could muster, Kat punched Baruch. She missed her intended target, but managed to strike him in the side.

If it affected him, he didn't show it. He just laughed as though they had just shared a joke.

"Oh, Katarina, you are going to be fun to break."

With that, Baruch wrapped his other hand around her neck and squeezed. Kat struggled and flung her arm and legs at him, but to no avail. He let go of her other arm as he lifted her off the ground, holding only her throat in a tight grip.

Flailing like a fish on the end of a hook, Kat struggled against his hold as he swung around and carried her across the room toward the bed. She kicked out with her legs, landing several blows to his stomach and ribs. He never even flinched.

She was done for. There was no way she could fight him.

When he reached the bed, the two women still reclining on the cushions pulled back the filmy drapes. Baruch tossed Kat onto the mattress. She bounced once like a rubber ball from the impact and then lay still, shaking her head, trying to clear it. She needed her wits about her if she was going to survive this. Either she was going to succumb to his will or she was going to die trying not to. She desperately hoped she'd get a chance to choose.

"Char, Haziel, grab her arms," Baruch commanded to the two scantily clad women kneeling next to Kat on the bed.

Before Kat could react, each woman took an arm and held them above Kat's head, pinning them to the mattress. Kat struggled, but they were both much stronger than she was. The best she could do was raise her shoulders and jerk them, sending jolts of pain down her arms and back.

Baruch grabbed one of her legs in each hand and spread them apart, so he could kneel in between. Once positioned, there was nothing she could do but squeeze him in a vise with her thighs. But she didn't think that would do anything but entice him further and spark more insistent throbbing in her loins.

Leering down at her, Baruch moved his hands up her thighs to rest on her pelvis. She could feel his heat emanating through his palms right through the leather of her pants.

"It would be better if you didn't fight me."

"Better for whom?"

Licking his lips, his gaze traveled from her face down to her crotch. She could see the elongated fangs peeking between his full, luscious mouth. "For you. I will enjoy it regardless, how much you struggle."

Kat wanted to scream but knew it would be pointless and futile. Not to mention a waste of energy that she was certainly going to need if she was going to escape. Although her situation seemed bleak, unavoidable, she wouldn't give up. If there were a way out, she'd find it.

Baruch leaned forward and covered her body with his own. Spreading out his legs, he was able to keep hers pinned to the bed and unable to kick him. Dipping his head, his mouth hovered over her breasts.

The women holding her arms giggled maliciously at Kat's plight. By the way their breathing increased, she could tell they were enjoying the show.

Kat could feel Baruch's hot breath through the cotton of her shirt. Clenching her teeth, Kat struggled against the urge to lift her chest to his waiting mouth.

He moved his face around, clearly taking in her scent with each deep intake of breath, but being careful not to touch her. "You can't stop the virus. It is racing through your bloodstream like a drug. Soon it will overpower you. You will be left helpless and weak, unable to resist the hungers eating at your insides." Closing his eyes, he pressed his slightly parted lips to her breast. She could feel the moisture of his tongue through her shirt. "A hunger for food, a hunger for sex, and a hunger for blood."

Kat drew her gaze away from him and glanced up at the two women holding her down. They both wore grins of feral satisfaction. Kat really wanted to smack those smiles off their pale faces. As she glared at the ghoulish woman on the left, Kat's eye caught a glimpse of something silver. Turning her head slightly, she could plainly see one of her knives strapped to the gaunt woman's thigh.

A flash of hope flared in her mind. Maybe the situation wasn't as desperate as it seemed. How could she get her knife? She needed use of her arms to be able to take back her weapon. But what would make the women release her?

Her attention swung back to Baruch. He watched her face as he teased her nipples with the tip of his tongue through the fabric. He was waiting for a reaction. She'd give him one.

Releasing her anger and the stranglehold she had on her desire, Kat let her body respond.

As soon as she made the decision, surges of pleasure crashed over her flesh, nearly drowning her in their power. She gasped as a hot flow of pleasure swept through her, pooling in a hot ball of intensity between her legs. It felt as if her pussy were on fire from the inside out. She groaned as Baruch bit down on her nipple.

"You see, it can be very pleasurable to give in to your desires," he growled as he released his biting clamp on her aching peak, and then moved over to do the same to her other one.

She writhed underneath him while he tortured her with exquisite piercing pain. Moving his hands up and under her shirt, Baruch wrapped his hands around her breasts and squeezed them, pushing her nipples up farther into his mouth.

Kat was never one for getting aroused by her pain, but what he was doing sent new violent jolts of pure bliss straight to her pussy. As the sensations increased deep inside, it became nearly unbearable, and she squeezed her thighs together, clamping down around Baruch's waist. Bucking her pelvis, she ground her sex into his. Anything to find release.

Baruch chuckled. "You will not find release that easily, Katarina. I will say when you will come." He relinquished his tight hold on her breasts and moved down her body so that his face was level with the crotch of her pants. Putting his nose right into the cross seam of her pants, Baruch took in a deep breath. "Mmm, you smell delicious. I bet you taste just as divine." He glanced up and smiled. "What do you think, Char? Would you like to play with our new friend here?"

The woman on the left giggled. "Oh, yes, please, my Lord. I think she's heavenly. So ripe and succulent, ready enough to eat."

Baruch moved his hand down to Kat's groin and pressed the palm against the crotch of her pants. Kat jerked from the shooting pangs of pleasure between her legs. Each time he pushed into her, the seam of the leather rubbed against her clit. The rough fabric on her sensitive nub nearly sent her spiraling headlong into an orgasm.

But before she could make the descent, Baruch removed his hand and the sensations vanished.

Kat gasped at the loss of pleasure. She was at his mercy. He could give or take whatever he wanted from her. She knew he would not send her into a climax too soon. He would first have his fun torturing her to the point of madness. Something needed to give, or she would not survive this with her mind or body intact.

Perhaps she had overestimated her power to resist Baruch.

He had somehow coaxed buried lusts in her to the surface. Erogenous zones she didn't realize existed popped up all over her body. Just the softest brush of his fingers on her belly, or his breath across her wrist, sent her blood boiling.

The virus racing inside was quickly taking over. Kat estimated that she had maybe ten more minutes before she gave in to the vicious battering of her senses. Her pussy felt like a ticking time bomb set to explode on Baruch's demand.

Baruch must have sensed her crumbling resolve as he slowly lifted up her shirt to expose her breasts. Blowing a soft breath across her nipples and flicking them with his tongue, he watched her face.

"Mmm, so close. So very close to giving in." He covered her nipple with his lips and sucked it into his mouth, rolling it back and forth between his teeth.

A sizzling whip of electricity shot through her body, starting at her breast, zinging over and through her belly, to end in a scorching ball of wetness between her thighs.

"Ah! Fuck!" Kat cried out as wave after hot wave of moisture gushed out of her to soak the crotch of her pants and dribble down her thighs. Every time Baruch sucked on her nipple, it was as if he were feasting on her pussy. If only he would, she thought. Then maybe she wouldn't feel like it was melting with the intense heat blazing from inside.

"Hmm, it seems you like that, don't you, my love?" Baruch chided as he switched nipples and started feasting on her left one, leaving her right in aching need.

"I want to play," Haziel, the woman on the right, whined. "It's not fair that we can't fuck her."

The moment she spoke, Kat could feel a lessening of pressure on her right arm. As Haziel bent forward to take part in the torture of Kat's breasts, Kat knew she had finally received her opportunity.

Battling back the constant throb of her pussy and the glorious hot flow of pleasure surging over her, Kat pushed all of her strength and energy into her arms. It was now or never.

With lightning-quick speed she didn't realize she possessed, Kat swung her right arm over her body and unsheathed the blade on Char's thigh. The unexpected movement startled Char and she released her tight hold on Kat's left arm. Without pause, Kat wrapped her left hand in Baruch's hair, tilted his head up, and pressed her knife to his throat. A trickle of blood ran down his neck where she had pushed the sharp blade into his flesh.

The two women started to shriek in protest.

"You bitches get off the bed or I will stick this blade through him and rip out his throat."

Before either one of the women could speak, Baruch assured them. "It's all right. Do as she says."

Char and Haziel reluctantly slid off the bed but stood nearby, both of them looking edgy and primed to jump at any moment. Kat knew they would do whatever Baruch demanded of them. She needed to be careful if this was going to work in her favor.

"You can't kill me, Katarina," Baruch purred as he raised his head up even farther and pushed up with his elbows on the mattress. The slight movements made Kat sit up with him, trying to keep her grip on his hair and the knife to his neck.

"The hell I can't. Keep moving and you'll see how fast I slit your throat."

"Do it, then. I won't stop you," he challenged as he kept moving up until he was on his knees.

Kat moved with him, until she, too, was kneeling. They were only an inch apart, and she could feel his hot breath on her face as he grinned.

She knew the second she drew the blade across Baruch's throat, his bitches would be on her with talons and teeth. But maybe in their blind rage, she could fight them off. She'd rather go down scrapping anyway. Living a long life was too over-rated.

"See you in hell, asshole."

The next few minutes felt like an eternity to Kat.

Before she could swipe her blade, she felt a pressure between her legs. Baruch had cupped her through her pants and was rubbing his hand hard over her crotch. Bolts of pleasure zinged up her body, giving pause to her hand.

Her hesitation cost her everything.

Quicker than she could think, Baruch punched her in the

sternum, sending her flying backward to smash into the concrete wall behind the bed. Before she fell, she managed to cut his chin open, but it wasn't enough. Baruch was still alive, and now he was pissed.

When she landed on the mattress facedown, she couldn't get her breath. The force of the blow had knocked all the wind out of her. Scrambling for air, she turned over onto her back and sucked in a breath. It burned all the way down her trachea and into her lungs like acid.

"Tsk, tsk, tsk." Baruch shook his head. Blood ran in rivulets down his chin to pool onto the sheets. "I expected more from you, Katarina. I never thought you'd be so foolish. If you were going to kill me, you should've done it the second you grabbed the knife." He grinned and the wound opened up like a sliced piece of beef. "Hesitation is weakness. Now you will pay for being so weak."

He nodded to Char and Haziel. With banshee shrieks, they launched themselves at Kat.

Kat felt the first few scratches and bites. She was past the point of numb when one of the Dweller women ripped open Kat's wrist and feasted on her blood.

Eventually everything went blissfully black. Thank the gods for small favors.

21

Pain shot through her head like thunderbolts as Kat blinked open her lids. Bright light shone harshly from above. She shut her eyes and groaned. Expecting them to be tied, Kat wriggled her arms. They were surprisingly unbound. She brought up a hand to her head and touched her skull gingerly. Her fingers came away sticky with blood. She didn't think her head could take much more. It had been beaten upon like a drum this time around. The pounding still reverberated inside.

She opened her eyes again and glanced around her surroundings. It didn't surprise her to see dank gray walls and smell the damp, stifling air. She had been seeing those walls and smelling that odor for a while now.

A wide slab of concrete lay like an altar in the middle of the room. She could just imagine what that was used for. She glanced up and noticed long, metal pipes lining the roof. The outsides were moist with condensation. She was deep underground in some kind of building, probably in the epicenter of the Vanquished City.

Kat shuffled her body and arranged her limbs that twisted

painfully under her. She was slumped against the wet wall of the empty room. Felt like she had just been tossed into the corner. From the aches and pains that screamed at her when she moved, it wouldn't surprise her if that was exactly what happened.

She moved and shuffled until she was leaning against the cement with her legs stretched out in front of her and her arms comfortably at her sides. Glancing down at her wrist, she remembered too well someone biting into her. The flesh still throbbed but, thankfully, the wound was scabbed over and healing rapidly.

One good thing about the Dark Dweller virus running rampant through the veins.

Tilting back her head, she moaned in agony. Sweat had popped out on her brow and lips from the exertion of moving. She couldn't remember ever feeling this beat-up. She was surprised she was still alive. And her stomach was rumbling. Loudly. Funny time to be thinking about food. But she was.

The thick metal door on the adjoining wall opened with a loud creak. Kat turned her head slightly but didn't move. She couldn't muster enough energy to do anything but blink. Even that sent jolts of pain to her skull.

A small, thin ratlike man shuffled into the room carrying a tray of food. The warm smell triggered contractions in her stomach. She cringed as her hunger gnawed at her insides.

He sneered as he neared her. Sharp, little kittenlike teeth peeked out between his pale, thin lips.

"You look hungry." He set down the metal tray on the cement floor an arm's length away. "Here's something to whet your appetite."

She glanced down at the food. It appeared to be a bowl of meaty stew, a piece of dry bread, and a cup of something dark. Tears sprung to her eyes as need encompassed her body. She reached out and dragged the tray closer.

The little man giggled as he shuffled out the door and pushed it shut.

Kat took the bread, dipped it into the stew, and took a healthy bite. She chewed and nearly choked. The bread was so dry, the juice from the stew couldn't make it soft. She picked up the cup and peered into it. It was dark red. She sniffed it. The tart aroma of wine wafted to her nose. She put it to her mouth, but hesitated.

She could smell something else under the cloying pungency. Something very familiar. She took another deep whiff and closed her eyes, savoring the scent.

Hades. She could smell him mixed in with the mulled wine.

Kat threw the cup across the room and screamed. "You fuckers! I'm going to rip every single one of you apart!" Angry tears welled in her eyes.

She picked up the bowl of stew and tossed it toward the door. It missed by miles, landing in an upturned mess on the floor. She kept the metal tray, thinking she could use it somehow. She hugged it to her chest just as the door creaked open again.

Little ratman shuffled in again. This time Baruch followed him, wearing a red robe. She must have gotten his black one dirty. He smiled as he entered, appearing to be enjoying a private joke. Another Dweller brought up the rear. A tall muscular woman with a shaved head.

"I see you've made a little mess," drawled Baruch.

"Yes, could you get the maid in here to clean it up?"

Baruch chuckled. The sound vibrated off the walls and wrapped itself around Kat. She winced while her heart skipped a beat. She refused to be attracted to him. But her body's betrayal was evident as her nipples tightened and her cunt began to tick just like a clock.

He moved across the floor as if floating to then stand in front of her. She tilted up her head to meet his gaze.

"You amuse me still, Katarina."

"And you make me fucking mad." She wanted to sit up, grab his leg, and bite into his thigh. The thought of his blood and flesh in her mouth sent shivers of delight over her body. Her gaze moved up his body and settled on the healing scar on his chin. She'd hurt him and now she had a feeling she was going to pay some more for that misdeed.

Baruch smiled and nodded at the rat man.

Both he and the bald woman moved to either side of Kat. They bent down and hooked her under the arms, yanking her to her feet. Pain exploded throughout her body as they dragged her to the cement block. Where one pain ended another enthusiastically picked up. Dizziness overcame her senses and she wanted to throw up.

They picked her up and tossed her down on her back onto the cement slab. Landing with a grunt on the hard, cold surface, new pains erupted in her spine. She had trouble forming any thoughts as her head swam in dark agony.

Baruch stood alongside, watching her with affection in his eyes. More like love of a pet then a person. He stoked a hand over her cheek and down to her mouth. He rubbed his fingers over her lips and pushed one in between.

Kat gagged as his finger probed her mouth. With her teeth, she clamped down around him.

Baruch flinched but grinned. "Yes. That's it. Bite into me. Make your transformation complete. Feed on my blood. Become one of us."

Kat relaxed her jaw. She would not give in, even if it meant letting him invade her.

Baruch withdrew his finger and wiped the spit on her torn, dirty shirt. "I thought the lesson you learned earlier would have been enough. You have amazing will, even now. I shall enjoy breaking it." He nodded to his companions. "I would have spared you this, Katarina, if you had accepted my offer. So in light of your refusal, I have no choice but to take what I want from you."

They left without a word, shutting the door behind them with a resounding thud. Kat was alone with him. In other circumstances, she would've been glad to be one-on-one with her captor, but in this case she knew it was the worst thing that could happen. If he were the only thing she had to concentrate on, her resolve would not last long. Already her stomach lurched in anticipation. Her thighs tingled and tightened at the thought of his exquisitely painful ways to make her succumb.

The jiggling of chains finally broke Hades out of his induced slumber. He blinked rapidly at his surroundings, although he knew exactly where he was. The dull throb in his arms solidified his answer as his body twisted slightly from the momentum of the dangling restraints. He was in the room from his dreams. Except, he was the one hanging naked from the ceiling in chains. His Dream Seer abilities had failed this time, thankfully. He didn't think he could handle seeing Kat hanging from the same fate.

He twisted his body so he could turn. He needed to see the others that he knew just by the smell alone were there. Four other bodies hung suspended from the roof. Not as many as he feared. Two were definitely dead. Eyes open, but no one looking through. The other two, one male and one female, appeared beaten and bloodied, but he could still see the shallow rise and fall of their chests.

Of the two of them, he studied the woman. He viewed her up and down and spied something familiar on her feet. There was thin webbing between her toes. Nemo's wife Kele. It was definitely her. Damnit! To his shame, he was hoping he and Kat wouldn't see her. Because now he couldn't leave without her. Not after all Nemo had done for them.

Hades swung back around. He had better start formulating a plan. If he hung there for very much longer, his arms would go numb and he would be useless to them all.

As he studied the machinations of his bindings, a tall, muscular woman with a shaved head stepped out of the shadows and into the sickly yellow light emanating from the fluorescents above. He nearly laughed. She looked exactly like him but as a woman.

She grinned as she neared his swaying body. "Hello, handsome. I'm Urzla. I get to keep you company while Baruch is busy doing your woman."

Hades cringed inside but he kept his outer appearance calm. He knew they wouldn't kill Kat. No, they wanted more from her than that. He just hoped he was strong and clever enough to get to her before she changed into something like the woman standing in front of him. Urzla was damn ugly, with bulging biceps, pale, translucent eyes, and long fangs poking out from between her pale lips. Hades hoped he never got that repulsive.

"Lucky me," he said, rolling his eyes.

She stood just out of reach of his legs and openly leered at his naked body. It didn't bother him in the least. He knew he was built well. She could stare at him all she wanted.

"Have you ever had blood drained out of your cock before?"

Hades flinched. Okay, now he was nervous.

"I can see by your face that you haven't had that experience yet." She grinned. "First I stroke you until you are nice and hard, then once you are thickly engorged with blood, I take just the tiniest of bites in the head and suck. Hard."

Hades could feel all the blood leave his head, and it wasn't going to his cock. He felt very faint.

She chuckled. "Trust me. You'll love it. That way you'll be primed and ready to go for when your woman comes to see you." She stepped toward him, a malicious grin on her angular face.

Lifting his legs, barely, Hades tried to pull back from her. The motion only caused him to start spinning. Within moments he felt a pair of warm, rough hands grabbing his legs and turning him around again. He tried to kick her but she held him still. She was incredibly strong, and because he had been hanging there for however long, his strength was draining from him.

"Fighting me will only make it more painful," she said as she eyed his cock and licked her lips.

"I'm impervious to pain, bitch. Give it your best shot."

With a low, rumbling growl, Urzla gripped his ass cheek, wrapped a hand around the shaft of his cock, and guided him into her gaping mouth.

When he slid past her plump lips, he could feel the scrape of her fangs on his sensitive flesh. Unfortunately, the feeling wasn't as unpleasant as he initially thought it would be. A man couldn't fight some things. A rumbling stomach and a woman sucking on his cock were on the top of the list.

Regardless of the woman, his cock quickly engorged with blood and became rock hard. With the way she was sucking him in to the base of his shaft, Hades didn't think it would take much for him to come. If he didn't do something quick, he would lose all his senses in his orgasm.

He wouldn't fail Kat that way.

Gritting his teeth against the onslaught of pleasure spearing him with each stroke of Urzla's mouth, Hades tried to lift his legs. He hoped she would be too enthralled with sucking his cock that she wouldn't notice the movement.

She didn't—not until his thighs were around her head.

Eyes wide, she tried to protest. His cock, thankfully, slid from her open mouth, and he was able to turn her around with a jerk of his legs. When she was nestled tightly at his crotch, Hades squeezed her as hard as he could.

She screamed and raged, clawing at his legs. But it was too late. He had her. With one powerful twist of his pelvis, he broke her neck. He opened his legs and she slumped to the cement floor, dead.

With a deep sigh Hades examined his chains and where they connected to the ceiling. *Now comes the tough part. Unhooking myself.* And he needed to do it quickly before any more Dwellers came by and noticed that his tormentor was lying dead at his dangling feet.

Kat swallowed audibly as the rat man wheeled in a metal tray with metal instruments neatly laid out on it. She'd never been tortured before. She'd been beaten, stabbed, even trampled by a horse, but never tortured for long periods. She had a high pain tolerance, but she didn't think she would be able to stand this. And it wasn't like she could just tell him a secret or some information to get him to stop. He wasn't torturing her for information.

Baruch was doing it for his own amusement.

He selected a long straight razor from his tools and held it above her body. Kat tried to move. She told her arms to lift up and knock the weapon from his hand. They didn't listen. All she managed was a jerk on her right shoulder as if she was shrugging to a question she couldn't answer.

He grinned down at her with an almost sympathetic twitch to his mouth. "Do not panic, my dear. I'm just simply removing your clothing. I can't sample your luscious body again when it's covered by filthy material, now, can I?"

Baruch gripped the collar of her T-shirt and sliced at the fabric. In one quick swipe the shirt was rendered in two. He gently laid aside the pieces, exposing her bare breasts to the cool air.

He gazed down at her fleshy orbs and sighed. "Exquisite."

"If you stop now, I might let you live," she said with as much bravado as she could muster.

Baruch laughed and shook his head. "That is exactly why I want you for my mate. You're so damn exciting. Isn't she fantastic, Sar?"

The little rat man nodded and leered down at her. "Yes, my Lord. Fantastic."

"You see, even Sar likes you. And Sar doesn't like anyone."

"I'm honored."

Baruch continued to chuckle as he grabbed hold of her leather pants. He frowned and then relinquished his grip. He set down the razor. "You know we needn't ruin these. We can just undo them and slide them down your legs. I might even let you have them back after we're done."

"How generous of you."

"You'd be surprised how generous I can be, Katarina." He slid his hand over her cheek and trailed it down to her breasts. He ran his fingers over her nipples, gently stroking them with each pass.

She shut her eyes against the treacherous waves of pleasure that washed over her. Her body was responding to him from deep inside. Whatever it was that raced wildly through her bloodstream recognized him. His smell. His touch. And it craved that connection desperately.

He moved his hand over her stomach to the zipper on her pants. He slowly pulled it down, opening the fly.

"Take her boots."

Sar moved to her feet and unbuckled her boots. He pulled them off, including her socks, and dropped them to the cement floor.

Kat fisted her hands at her sides as Baruch slowly pulled her pants down. He had some trouble as her skin was slick with sweat, but he managed to slide them down her legs with minimal effort. He dropped them onto the floor next to her boots.

As he moved up to her side, he trailed his fingers over her legs with feathery touches. Kat clenched her jaw, trying desperately not to moan. It was nearly impossible to fight the sensations that assaulted her body. Her mind told her she didn't want this. That this man was a filthy creature of the sewers. But her body yearned for him. For his light or rough touch. Her cunt ached with every flicker of his finger, with every breath from his lips. She was in a vibrating state of arousal and had no way to fight it. If only he would end her suffering and give her release, she could still assimilate her senses and muster enough strength to escape. But she knew he would never make it that easy.

Baruch hummed as his fingers neared her sex. He brushed them lightly against her mound and then continued up her body. He swept them over her nipples again but with harder, swift strokes. He squeezed one between his thumb and index finger, rolling it back and forth.

"I see behind your eyes that you still think you can escape." He tugged hard on her nipple. She winced and moaned lightly.

"But I will not let you think, Katarina. I will do anything I want to you so that you can't think, but only feel . . . me. Then and only then will I release you."

Baruch reached over to the tray and picked up two metal clamps with a little length of string attaching them together.

"You'd be surprised what we've been able to find over the years. Things from our past. Instruments of exquisite pleasure to me." He held them over her breasts. "And to you, my dear, Katarina."

Kat watched in awe as Baruch attached one clamp and then the other to her nipples. She felt the pressure and pleasures instantly. He watched her face intently as he adjusted the force on each nub. She squirmed under the sensations that thrilled her body. Each nipple sent jolts of pleasure zinging down her body, settling in deep within her cunt. She could feel herself getting wetter and wetter as the tension on her rigid peaks increased.

Baruch grinned as she grimaced in rapture. "You see the delight I bring you? Why fight me so hard? I could promise you a lifetime of this and more."

He twirled the string around his index finger and tugged on it, pulling on her nipples. Kat bowed her back as surges of rapture washed over her. She moaned loudly as her cunt began to throb under the crashing waves of pleasurable torment.

He held out his hand toward Sar. The little rat man picked up another metal clamp from the tray. This one was longer, about three inches, with little beads hanging from the end. Kat tried to get her mind around its purpose. But she could hardly think while Baruch continued to tug at her nipples.

"I find this little instrument very interesting." He grinned as he let go of the string on her tit clamps.

He moved down to her sex. He brushed at her mound like petting an animal. He slid his finger into her cleft and twirled it around.

"You are so wet, my dear. I fear that this will take you over the edge. I will go slowly so that you do not."

With his finger and thumb, he spread her inner folds. He positioned the clamp over her, opened the clamp, and slid it down into her cleft. He found her clit easily, as it was swollen and begging to be touched.

Kat sucked in a ragged breath as he slid the clamp over her aching nub. He closed the arms around it, pinching it in between. Spears of pleasure stabbed her body. She could hardly breathe as jab after jab of sensations pierced her flesh.

He chuckled. "I see that you like my new toy." He pulled on her nipples again. "If you surrender to me, you could experience this at your leisure and mine, of course."

Kat wanted to move off the cement block. She wanted to reach down and pull the clamp off her clit. She didn't want to delight in his tortures. She didn't want to beg him for more.

Squeezing her eyes shut against the barrage of rapture, Kat prayed that she could resist him. Surrender sounded more and more savory by the minute.

Static crackled overhead from speaker in the wall. "Lord Baruch, we have a problem in the chain room."

Baruch frowned and withdrew his hand from Kat's sex, pulling off he clamp. She groaned and writhed in regret. She was almost there. One more pinch on her clit and she was sure to explode.

While he wiped his hand on his robe, he addressed Sar. "Keep her entertained, but no fucking. That is my privilege alone."

"Yes, my Lord."

Kat watched at Baruch left, noticing that he didn't shut the door all the way. She turned back to Sar, her body still humming from arousal and near climax. Even the breeze from the open door caused ripples of pleasure over her flesh.

Sar leered down at her, drool dribbling from the side on his thin mouth. She grimaced and turned her head away.

"You've got me horny as a bull." He touched her gingerly as if touching a revered religious idol. "I can't put my dick in your cunt." He moved his hand over her mound, dipping his fingers into her hot, slick cleft. "But he didn't say anything about putting it in your mouth."

Sar brought his hand up to her mouth, rubbing his wet fingers over her lips. Kat licked them eagerly. She needed release now. She couldn't go another minute without it. She grabbed his other hand. He flinched at her sudden movement but didn't pull away as she dragged them down to her cunt.

She bent her legs and spread them wide apart, placing his fingers at her clit. Her voracity gave strength back to her limbs. She put her hand on top of his and guided him to just the right spot. She pushed his fingers down hard onto her swollen, achy nub and moved it quickly back and forth. Sar groaned as she continued to suck on his fingers and guide his hand on her cunt.

"Ooh, bitch, you are something else."

Kat could feel her orgasm peak. She closed her eyes against the intense surge of pleasure that pounded into her. She moaned loudly against the fingers in her mouth. Her legs and whole body shook with delight. It felt like molten lava gushing out of her and over her hand. In that one moment as the heated sensations of her orgasm poured over her, she felt herself go. It was as though she were floating on a white, fluffy cloud in the brilliant blue sky. She felt at peace. Seemingly, the two warring sides in her body had finally signed a truce.

Sar tried to pull his fingers out of her mouth. But she continued to suck on them hard. "Careful there, wouldn't want to bite me."

Kat squeezed her eyes shut and clamped her teeth around his digits. She bit down hard. Hot, salty blood spurted into her mouth. It tasted like sugar as it dribbled down her dry throat.

Sar screamed and yanked his hand away. He was minus two fingers and counting. He cradled his bloody hand to his chest. "You stupid bitch! You're going to change now."

Kat sat straight up and smirked, her lips smeared crimson. "Hey, I needed a change anyway."

She moved her legs quickly, spinning around and kicking Sar in the head. He stumbled back but didn't fall. Kat jumped off the cement block and rushed at him. Along the way she filched the razor from the metal cart.

Two well-placed swipes later, Sar lay on the cement floor, bleeding . . . badly. Kat grabbed her pants and boots, putting them back on. After removing the nipple clamps, she tore off the rest of her shirt. It was useless. She glanced down at Sar and smiled. His tank top was red now and ripped in one place, but it would do.

Fully dressed and armed with a straight razor, Kat moved to

the door and peeked out. The passageway was empty. She had
to find Darquiel and get her to show the location of the
Monolith. She had come this far and she wasn't leaving without
it. By the sounds of the commotion in the chain room, she assumed Hades had escaped. That suited her fine because now
she wouldn't have to worry about him and she could do what
she came for.

Hades crept down a deserted passageway with Nemo's wife
slung over his shoulder. He needed to find a way up, take her
out, and come back down for Kat. He wouldn't leave without
her.

As the passageway opened up into a large open area, Kele
started to mumble incoherently. The woman had been through
more than he could ever imagine. According to Nemo, she had
been taken over a month ago. That was a long time to be in the
sadistic hands of the Dwellers.

Hades murmured to her quietly and continued. A steep set
of metal stairs was at the end of the room. They went up to another level. That was all he cared about. Up was good.

He held her tightly and ran through the room. Just as he
reached the stairs, he felt a presence behind him. He whipped
around, the knife he confiscated from Urzla in his hand.

"What are you wearing?" Kat stood there, a hand on her
hip, staring at him.

He sighed and closed his eyes. *Oh, thank the gods*, he thought.
He grinned and glanced down at himself. After disposing of
Urzla with a twist of his powerful legs, Hades had taken off her
pants and shirt. He couldn't be running around naked now,
could he?

One problem was that neither of them fit too well. She was a
big girl, but he was larger. The pants fit around the waist but
were too short. The hem came to midcalf and the shirt was tight
and constricting, showing off his rippled abdominal muscles.

He laughed but it soon faded when he really noticed her. "You're covered in blood. Where are you hurt?"

Kat shook her head. "Relax, it's not mine."

He studied her closely. Somehow she didn't look the same. Her face seemed paler and her eyes darker. Even her cloudy one. Could be the trick of the waning light, but he didn't think so. She was different.

"Did they hurt you? I feared the worse."

"Nah, nothing I couldn't handle. Besides, I took a bite out of them before they could do anything worse."

Hades froze as he realized the truth behind her flippant comment. She had taken blood. The change was upon her. He had been too late to save her.

"Don't look at me like that. I'll deal with it. Let's just do what we came to do and get the fuck out of here."

"Okay, let's take her out and then come back."

She shook her head. "No, if we leave we'll never get back down. They'll have guards all over the place."

"What do we do with her? I won't leave her."

"Take her out. Get somewhere safe. I'll get the Monolith and meet you topside."

"We shouldn't split up."

"Don't you trust me?"

Hades grabbed her arm and pulled her to him. "I do trust you. That's not why I don't want to split up."

When she looked at him, he spied something like regret on her face. Hades could see the war within her. The one between her heart and her mind.

"Take her out, Hades. You're the hero in this tale. Save her."

"And who are you in this?"

"The tragic heroine with several character flaws and counting."

Hades chuckled softly. He knew what she was doing. Making

it easier on him to leave. But no matter what she did, it would not be easy.

He nodded and leaned down to press his lips to hers. She turned her head at the last moment and he pressed his mouth to her cheek. He nuzzled into her hair, whispering into her ear.

"I love you, Hell Kat. No matter what, always remember that."

She pulled away from him and nodded. As she turned to go back, Hades swore he saw tears running down her cheeks. But it could have been the trick of the waning light. He shuffled Nemo's wife on his shoulder and began climbing up the metal stairs. With each step he took, the feeling of loss overwhelmed him. He feared he would never see Kat again.

22

Kat crept down another dark passageway. This was the second she had passed without running into anyone. She found that very disturbing since they had both escaped. Wouldn't they be crawling all over searching for them? She was certain that Baruch would not let them go so easily. So where was everyone?

She really needed to find Darquiel. But she knew that was almost impossible. Like finding a mouse in a maze. Maybe, if she relaxed and opened herself, she could touch her mind. If Baruch felt Darquiel and she could feel him, then maybe Kat could touch Darquiel. Darquiel had made Damian, who had made Kat. She supposed it was worth a shot.

Slinking down into a crouch against the cement wall, Kat took a deep breath and closed her eyes. She needed to empty her mind. Or so she assumed. It made sense that she would be more susceptible to psychic links if her mind was free of fear and thought . . .

Blinding white pain squeezed her brain.

She clamped her hands over her ears and curled into a ball

on the floor. It felt as though her head were going to explode from the pressure inside. Dark, incoherent images flashed behind her eyes. They flashed over and over in a repeated pattern. It felt as though she were being blinded from the inside out.

It stopped abruptly and Kat opened her eyes. White spots floated in her vision, but, thankfully, she could still see. She took in some deep breaths, willing her heart to slow from its frantic pounding.

She had touched something. Several somethings. One had been very big. She couldn't see it, but got a sense of its size just from the pressure it drove into her mind. And she had touched something very familiar.

Damian. He was here and alive.

Kat pushed herself up to stand. Her legs wobbled, but she stood firm. She started down the passageway, moving toward the "feelings" lingering in her mind. She had a sense that Damian was waiting for her down the way.

She crept down the passage, on guard for anything. Soon it ended and opened up into another large area. The smell hit her immediately. A dank, putrid odor not unlike the smell of animal feces.

She stepped across the room quietly and slowly. She scanned the area as she moved, but there were too many dark corners and shadows to be able to see everything. As she moved into the center of the room, she had a sense of something shuffling in the corner by a tall metal pillar. She stopped and peered into the dark.

A soft growl erupted from the shadows. It wasn't a deep growl—more like a loud rolling of the tongue. She wondered what would make that kind of sound, but didn't want to stick around to find out. Kat ran across the room toward the exit.

A large green animal stepped out of the shadows and into a beam of light. Kat gasped and skidded to a halt. It scampered toward her, but was pulled back by the metal chain that teth-ered it to the post.

Kat had never seen or read about anything like it. It had dark mossy-green, shiny skin like a snake. And it was big even as it hunkered down on all fours like an obedient dog. To Kat, it looked like an overgrown lizard with thin-slatted, red eyes. As it pulled on its restraint and whined like a sad puppy, Kat noticed it also had wings. They were tucked securely into its thick body.

It was a mutated animal of some sort. Combinations of traits from different species like a reptile and a bird formed this crea-ture. As Kat watched it, she realized it meant her no harm. She had touched this creature in her mind. It had left a feeling of sadness and despair in her head. It was a prisoner just like her.

She took a step toward it, her hand held out. "Hey, there, Ugly, whatcha in for?"

The creature cocked its head to one side as if in question. Its little ears on the top of its head flickered.

Kat frowned. "Can you understand me?"

The creature nodded its large head.

"Holy—"

She was hit from the side and taken down to the floor. Her assailant rolled them across the room. She knocked him in the head with her fist.

"Damnit, Hades. It wasn't going to hurt me."

"How do you know?"

"Because I can feel it in my head. It's scared."

Hades rolled off her and scrambled to his feet. He offered her his hand and pulled her up.

"What are doing here? Where's the woman?"

"I took her up. I found this mechanical box that went all the way to the top. I hid her in another building. It's midday, so I don't think any dwellers are top side."

"I told you to get safe."

"Yeah, yeah. You sure are bossy."

Kat smiled. She didn't want to admit it, but she was elated that he had come back.

"Now what?" Hades asked.

"We find the Monolith and get the fuck out of here. And I know just how to do that." She walked back to the creature. Hades followed her hesitantly.

"What is that thing?"

"It's a mutant of some sort. Its how they've been getting around at night. How they surprised us out on the limits. They're using it to fly."

She reached out to touch it. The creature shied away and then sniffed the air. It rolled its tongue again and inched its head forward. Kat touched its nose gently. It pushed its nose into her hand, appearing to want more of her affections.

"Okay, so we have our transportation; how do we get the Monolith?" Hades asked.

"I'm not sure. I tried to feel for Darquiel but didn't find her. I found someone else though."

"Who?"

"Damian. He's alive and in this building somewhere."

"Shit. That complicates matters."

"Yup."

His eyes searched her face. "It's your call."

"I can't leave him here."

"Okay. So let's see," Hades reiterated, "we have to find Darquiel so she can help us find the Monolith. Probably have to kill a bunch of Dwellers to get to it. Then we find Damian, run back here, jump on the birdie, and fly out."

"Yup, sounds about right."

"Great, all we have to do now is run into Lord Ghoul himself and we'd have a perfect plan."

Kat's hand stilled on the creature. She closed her eyes and swore. "Fuck."

"What?"

"We meet again. How wonderful."

Hades and Kat turned around just as Baruch and two of his goons stepped out of the shadows.

"And we're all here like just one big, happy family."

Darquiel stepped out of the dark and stood beside Baruch, and on the other side, Damian stepped into the light.

Kat flinched when she saw him. He looked badly beaten. His face was cut up, and both eyes were black and green. He seemed to be favoring his right leg and his side. She wasn't sure if it was the twister that had torn him up or Baruch.

Baruch smiled and put his hand on Damian's shoulder. "We found him tossed away like garbage not far from here. Poor boy has had quite the trip." He moved his hand over Damian and through his hair. Damian tried to pull away but Baruch held him still.

Kat noticed the battle. She cheered inside that Damian still had some fight left in him. Hopefully it would be enough to get them out of there.

"Damian, is it here?" Kat inquired.

"Yes."

"You must be talking about the Monolith." Baruch released his hold on Damian, watching Kat the entire time. She could feel the weight of his gaze on her. It felt oppressive like the humidity outside in the hot sun. "Yes, Katarina, I have it here. See for yourself."

He stuck out his arm and opened his hand.

Kat motioned to Hades. He looked just as confused as she was. How could the Monolith be in his hand? How could the most important piece of technology be contained in the palm of the hand?

She took a step forward. Hades grabbed her arm and shook his head. "It's a trick."

"No, I assure you, dear Hades, it is not. I hold the key to the entire future of our people and the demise of the old in my hand. Amazing, isn't it?"

Kat's gaze swung to Damian. He nodded his head at her silent question. It was not a trick. The Monolith, the key to her freedom, was right in front of her. She just had to reach out and grab it. And probably kill three people to keep it. But, hey, nothing was free.

As she moved forward, Kat glanced at Darquiel. The girl watched her with an eyebrow raised. Was that a sign? Or a warning?

Right before Kat could peer into Baruch's hand, Darquiel grabbed the ax the other goon held and swung it toward Kat. Kat yelped and jumped back just as the blade sliced through Baruch's wrist. Involuntarily his hand clenched as it fell to the ground, the Monolith encased safely inside his fist.

Kat scooped up the severed hand and turned back to Hades and the winged creature. "C'mon, Damian! Let's go!"

Damian broke out of his stupor and started running. He grabbed Darquiel's arm as he passed, dragging her with him.

While he cradled his bloodied arm to his chest, Baruch screamed. His guards were in too much shock to do anything but stare at their injured leader.

"Kill them!" Baruch shrieked.

To Kat it seemed like slow motion while they ran to their transport. Damian and Darquiel ran hand in hand next to her. She turned and looked at them as they sprinted across the room.

Hades stood waiting with the creature. "Throw me the ax!" he demanded at Darquiel.

She tossed it to him. Kat watched it sail through the air.

Hades caught it on the fly, turned, and broke through the chain that imprisoned the beast.

It reared up and extended its leathery wings. Hades took hold of its collar and grabbed Kat's arm, hefting them both onto its scaly back. Damian and Darquiel both jumped, their arms extended. They managed to catch hold of the beast's ridged spine and hang on as the creature flapped its wings and lifted them into the air.

By the time the two Dwellers snapped into action and jumped up after them, it was too late. The beast kicked his hind feet back and caught them in midair, sending them flying to the ground.

Damian and Darquiel scrambled onto its back and settled in behind Kat. Kat watched the ground pull away as the beast rose. Baruch stood still in the middle of the room, blood dripping onto the floor, and hell-bent rage contorting his pale face.

Kat sighed and closed her eyes. She could feel his anger in her head and in her body. It felt like a ball of liquid fire roaring through her insides. She flinched from the pain, and the severed hand tumbled from her grip.

Reaching blindly for it, she fell over onto her side. Hades snatched her arm before she could fall. The hand bumped the side of the beast and tumbled off. Kat cried out as she watched her future fall.

But it was snatched up before it could drop. Darquiel held it deftly in her hand as she hung upside down from the beast's back. Damian clutched her legs as she dangled. She shuffled backward and handed the hand to Kat. Kat took it and hugged it to her body.

"Thank you."

Darquiel just nodded and snuggled into Damian's arms and closed her eyes.

When they had reached the top level, Kat could not see a way out. "Now what?"

The beast reached out with his taloned claw and pushed a large red button on the wall. Sirens blared and crimson lights swirled around in dazzling color. The metal roof above them began to slide open. Kat smiled as the first rays of the sun glared down on them.

When the door fully opened, the beast swooped into the sky. Kat laughed and wrapped her arms around Hades.

"We need to pick up Kele and then we'll head home. Shouldn't take long with this thing," Hades said.

Kat nodded and pressed her head into his back. Home. That was a word she hadn't thought of in a long time. Home had always meant family and love to her. She had been without both for so long.

Snuggling in closer to Hades, she wondered if this was something she could have again.

23

Russell touched the hand reverently, his eyes wide and brimming with tears. She could see the hesitation in his face, and wondered why. This was it. This was the one thing he had been waiting for his whole life. She supposed she understood as her stomach lurched over again. This was the one thing she had been searching for her whole life, and she wasn't too sure she was quite ready for it.

As if sensing her mood, Hades put an arm around her and pulled her close. She snuggled into him.

Russell pried open the fingers one by one. He sighed loudly as he gazed down into the palm. In the middle lay a tiny metal square. Russell touched it with his fingertip and brought it up to his face. He pulled the magnifying glass attached to his head over to his eye. He gazed down at it through the glass.

He sighed. "There it is. The future."

"But what is it?" Hades asked.

"A computer microchip. This one tiny thing has the power to control our entire destiny."

"Ah, okay. So how much are you going to give us for our destiny?"

Russell chuckled as he set the tiny chip on a piece of glass on his counter. He took off his headgear and eyed Kat and Hades.

"How much do you need?"

"Enough to buy us a piece of property up north, and a couple of bikes, and some left over to buy a couple of luxuries, like a shave." Hades rubbed a hand over the growth on his chin and turned to Kat. "What do you think, babe? Is that enough?"

She shrugged, turning from his gaze. "Sounds about right." She didn't want him to see what was in her mind.

Russell turned, bent down, and slid open a shelving door. A black safe lay nestled inside. He turned the lock and opened it. Reaching in, he came away with a large leather purse and set it on the counter in front of them. It jingled as it moved.

"Will this be enough?" He laughed.

Hades and Kat went to the tavern and dined on steak and fresh vegetables. They drank a bottle of vodka and watched the entertainment.

It was a night for celebration. But Kat did not feel celebratory. She felt empty and cold inside. As if she had been hollowed out with a spoon like a pumpkin at Hallows' Eve. The virus had contaminated her. And changed her into someone else. Someone she was uncertain she could live with.

Hades's voice startled her from her somber musings.

"Damian said their trip was quick. Riding Ugly has its advantages. Nemo sends his blessings, and Leucothea kept asking about you."

"That's great," she said absently while she sipped her drink.

"They'll meet us up north in a few weeks."

"Okay."

Hades reached across the table and gripped her hand. "What's up?"

She startled out of her daze and regarded him. Maybe for the first time. He was the sexiest man she had ever laid eyes on. And he was just and honest. Two things that surprised her to no end. He was the perfect man for her.

She got up, still holding his hand, and settled onto his lap. She straddled him, wrapped her arms around his neck, and nuzzled into his ear.

"Take me home, Hades. I want to feel *you* inside of me."

Hades lifted her up, his hands over her ass, and carried her out of the tavern.

He carried her all the way to the apartment like that, cradled against his body, her head resting on his broad shoulder.

Kat moaned as Hades laid her down on the bed. He stripped off her shirt in one deft motion. He sat at her feet and unbuckled her boots, tossing them over his shoulder. He undid her pants and slid them down her legs, all the while watching her face.

He stood up on the bed and stripped off his clothes. She laughed as he struggled with his leather pants. His foot caught in the cuff and he fell over onto the mattress. Kat rolled over and gladly helped him off with his pants.

As she slid in next to him, she pressed kisses to his body, starting at his stomach and making her way up his powerful chest to his face. She pressed her mouth to his and kissed him passionately, dipping in her tongue to taste him. To savor his flavor.

He wrapped his hands in her hair and rolled her over, covering her with his powerful body. He spread her legs with his knee and settled in between them.

As he lifted himself to sink his cock into her hot, wet opening, he cupped her face in his hands. He turned her head so that she was looking at him. Only him.

"You are the only treasure I ever wanted," he whispered.

Tears fell from her eyes as he stretched her open and filled her up. Kat didn't want to feel this way about Hades. She didn't want the intense way he considered her to matter. But it did. He mattered. More than any man she'd ever known.

Wrapping her arms around him, she held on as he took her up with each stroke of his cock. Ripples of pleasure flowed over her and she gasped at their intensity. Only Hades could make her feel so many things. With him sheathed inside, she was acutely aware of every nerve ending tingling, every spot on her skin quivering from his briefest touch. She could smell all his scents, the sweat trickling down his skin, the musk of his cock, the vodka on his breath, the blood racing through his veins and down to his groin.

She dug into his flesh with her nails as her body roared to life like an out-of-control bonfire. Hot, scorching flames of desire licked at her insides. She squirmed and bucked underneath Hades, urging him to go deeper. To douse the intense sensations with the pounding of his cock.

Burying her face into the side of his neck, Kat closed her eyes against the onslaught of extreme sensations crashing over her. But the moment she did, she could hear the pumping of his blood through the veins in his throat and knew she had made a grave error. Opening her eyes, she watched as the flesh on his neck pulsed rhythmically with the force of his racing heart.

Desperation clawed at her. A powerful craving to sink her teeth into that blood reservoir swept through her, causing her stomach to clench with hunger. She could already taste the metallic tang on her tongue. It would be like candy, she thought.

Squeezing her eyes shut, she tried to force the feelings aside. She would not let Hades be the first victim of the Dark Dweller virus possessing her body and mind. She loved him too much.

Love? Is that what she truly felt for him? Opening her eyes, she stared at him as he pounded into her, his face a mask of determination and feeling. Yes, she could truly say that she loved him. For the first time in her life, she felt love—true, honest, and unconditional—for another human being. With that realization she was able to push back the creeping feelings of hunger and blood lust.

But it wouldn't last long.

"Stop, Hades," she panted, pushing at his shoulders.

Pausing, confusion furrowing his brow, he asked, "What's wrong?"

"I can't do this."

"What? Why?"

"I just can't."

Hades cupped her cheeks with his hands, forcing her to look at him when she wanted to turn away. "Tell me why."

With an angry sigh, she snapped, "Because I want to rip open your throat and drink your blood. Is that reason enough?"

He stared at her for several seconds before he responded. "Hey, babe, lots of women have wanted to do that to me before. I don't take those threats seriously."

"Take this one seriously, Hades. It's not a joke." The flare of anger was not helping her increasing hunger. It gave it an erotic edge. One she really wanted to sample. She pushed at him again. "We can't do this. It's not worth it. I'll end up killing you in the end."

"But it *is* worth it. Can't you see that, Kat? All the reasons you think are dangerous are exactly the reasons why this is so good." He pressed his lips to hers. "Because I know you won't kill me. I won't let you. I love you too much to let that happen."

Damn him! He knew her too well. With tears brimming in her eyes, Kat wrapped her hands around his head and kissed him. Her tongue dived into his mouth and swept over his in an effort to take him all in, to implant his flavor forever into her mind. His words moved her in ways she had never experienced before. Her heart felt as though it were in a vice, being squeezed of all its contents. Love was certainly the most painful emotion a person could ever suffer. With it came everything else: grief, loss, jealousy, anger—emotions Kat never thought she'd know again. Not after the loss of her entire family. And here they all were again, bottled up into one man.

A man she realized she would die for.

As they kissed and Hades began to swell again inside her, Kat could feel the virus flaring again. This time it was in a violent rage. Instant sensations of blood lust surged over her and she dug her nails deep into his shoulders. The sharp tang of blood floated to her flaring nostrils.

"Hades," she growled, "I can't control it much longer."

"Flip over."

"What?"

"Trust me."

Kat did as he asked and turned over onto her stomach. As she did, she felt him leave the mattress.

"Grab the spokes on the headboard."

Hesitant, she gripped two metal spindles on the headboard. The moment she did, Hades was there with a length of rope and had tied her wrists to them—tightly with double knots. Instinct told her to struggle against the restraint, but she understood his reasons, and let him do it. He was smart, her man.

"There now, you can't scratch or bite me." He chuckled. "And now I can fuck you for the rest of the night without being interrupted. That should satisfy your hungers."

Glancing over her shoulder, she sneered as he pulled her legs apart and settled in between them. "Well, hurry up, then. I'm starting to dry up inside."

She moaned as Hades parted her labia with his thumbs. Slowly he slid his finger deep into her opening.

"Liar."

With a sigh Kat closed her eyes as Hades continued to stroke her pussy. In between long, languid thrusts with his fingers, he slid along her cleft and rubbed at her clit.

Wave after wave of pure pleasure rolled over her, keeping the other depraved hungers at bay. *For the time being*, she thought. It would take more than a few well-placed fingers to fight her blood lust.

Appearing to read her thoughts, Hades positioned himself between her thighs and gripped her hips, pulling her to her knees. The movement spread her legs farther apart and opened her sex wide. The breeze from the open window tickled her exposed flesh, eliciting shivers that cascaded over her body.

"I love you like this, Hell Kat. Open, waiting, vulnerable. And mine."

With that, he thrust his cock into her, ramming it to the hilt in one singular move.

She cried out as he ground himself into her with wide pelvic circles. She could feel and hear his balls slapping against her cleft. Tilting up her ass, she urged him for more. She wanted, needed more of him. Even with him buried deep inside her pussy, she felt empty. She knew that the virus was burning her up inside, dissolving like acid everything decent inside her. She needed Hades to fill her up with something else. Anything else, to fulfill the void that was slowly taking over.

"More. Harder. Faster," she panted as she bit down on the blanket on the bed and pushed against him.

As Hades increased his tempo, Kat could feel him probing her anus, sliding his fingers down to where her entrances joined and then back up again, rubbing her lubricating juices over her crevice. With slow, careful movements, he pushed one long, meaty finger into her.

"Ah, fuck yes," she groaned, grinding against his hand.

With her encouragement, he slid another finger into her tight opening. As he pumped his fingers in and out, he continually rammed his cock into her. She was taking a pounding and she loved it. She'd never before been so stuffed. Hades's cock was so thick and long, she could almost feel it in her throat each time he thrust forward.

She was very close to coming. A few accurate flicks on her swollen, aching clit and she'd explode. Too bad her hands were tied or she'd take care of it herself.

"Jesus, woman, you feel so fucking good," Hades grunted as he buried himself deep and stayed there, moving his pelvis in short, quick bursts.

While his one hand fiddled with her anus, he reached around her hip and slid his fingers into her inner folds. He found her clit and rubbed at it hard. Quick, sharp spears of ecstasy zinged up and down her body when he pinched her sensitive nub between his finger and thumb. That's all it took.

Every muscle in her body started to quiver. A hot, boiling ball of pleasure erupted inside her belly and radiated down into her pussy. She cried out as her orgasm slammed into her. Small bursts like explosions erupted all over her body. She had never felt anything remotely like it as her head spun and white, blinding light flashed behind her eyes.

Only seconds later, Hades joined her. With one powerful thrust, plunging his cock as deep as he could, he emptied himself inside her. Kat could feel her pussy tighten around him, milking him dry with each contraction.

Gasping for air, Kat collapsed onto the mattress. Hades went down with her, his cock still imbedded deep within her sex. As they lay there, their breathing labored, sweat still trickling down their bodies, Kat could barely think past her trembling form. Her mind was blank. And she thanked Hades for that. She couldn't feel the virus.

"Did it work?" Hades asked, his voice muffled from the side of her neck.

"Yes."

"Good." He chuckled. "Now, that won't be too bad to do every time you feel it rising, will it?"

She laughed with him. "No, that won't be too bad."

The virus lay dormant inside her. She could still feel it, sense it stirring deep inside. Although sex with Hades had controlled it this time, she knew one day that their love would not be strong enough to contain it. And she sensed that that day was coming soon.

But for now she would enjoy the afterglow of their love-making. And maybe a little more.

"Untie me," she growled. "I'm not nearly done with you."

Hades raised himself from her back and glanced down at her face. "Is it safe?"

"For now."

Kat rolled over and peeked at Hades. He was sleeping with his arms and legs spread across the bed. She carefully pulled her arm out from under him and sat up on the edge of the bed. She gathered her clothes and dressed in silence.

Their lovemaking had been perfect. He had made it that way, especially for her. It was honest, beautiful, and true. That was why she hurt so badly inside. Because she was no longer any of those things. Or ever could be.

She glanced once more at Hades and reached over to touch his face. As a last reminder of his touch.

He opened his eyes and grabbed her hand. "Where're you going?"

She could feel the tears welling in her eyes again. She sucked them back and tried to keep from shaking.

"Out."

He stared into her eyes, searching for something. He finally released her hand and let his arm fall in defeat.

"Be safe."

"I will."

Kat couldn't handle the way he studied her, as if privy to her most secret thoughts. She hoped he understood but couldn't blame him if he didn't. She leaned on the bed and covered his mouth with hers, kissing him softly, tenderly.

"You are everything I ever wanted in a man, in a partner." She moved her mouth over his face and pressed her lips to his forehead. She wanted to stay there, pressed against him, breathing in his scent. "But you smell too damn good," she murmured into his skin.

She closed her eyes against the tears and walked out of the room.

"I'll be up north if you need me."

Without looking back, she sucked in a breath and walked out the apartment door.

Outside, she jumped on her bike and kicked it over. She wiped at her eyes for the last time and slipped on her skullcap. She glanced up at the apartment window. But Hades wasn't there.

She'd see him again, she hoped. There was just something she needed to do first. She needed to control the beast inside. Until then she couldn't let herself love anyone. And not kill them in the end.

A thundering flap of air hit her in the face. She glanced up into the sky and saw a dark shape swooping in the sky above her. She smiled. At least she'd have company on her journey, even if it were a big, ugly mutated beast.

She booted the up stand and revved the bike. She turned right down the back alley and onto the main road out of town. Pulling on the handle to kick up the speed, Hell Kat rode out of town and into the blossoming sunrise.

Here's a hot sneak peek at
AFTER HOURS,
by Jodi Lynn Copeland.
Available now from Aphrodisia . . .

There was something to be said about the way a woman danced. Between her body-hugging, short red dress and the arousing way she twisted her sleek curves, the woman who currently held Brendan Jordan's attention seemed to be saying "do me" loud enough to be heard halfway across the hotel reception hall.

He glanced over at Mike Donovan, his one-time college roommate and the newest victim of matrimony, then nodded toward the blonde.

From his seat next to Brendan at the head table, Mike followed Brendan's gaze. His grin turned from one of newly married idiocy to that of male understanding. "Pretty incredible, isn't she?" he asked loudly, to be heard over the blaring music.

Drool-worthy was a more suitable way to describe her. Only, Brendan didn't drool over women. If anything, the situation was reversed. They gave him the hot, hungry, fuck-me looks that made it clear what they wanted even before they approached. And, if they were lucky, he gave it to them.

The blonde wasn't drooling over him. Judging by the dreamy

expression that tugged her slightly too wide mouth into one of the sexier smiles he'd seen, she wasn't even aware there were other people in the room.

Brendan was aware, however. Aware of how damned long he'd been sitting there ogling her. Looking away, he took a long pull from his beer. He set the bottle back on the table before nonchalantly asking, "So, who is she?"

Mike's eyebrows rose. "You haven't met Jilly?"

"That's her name?" Brendan gave the woman an assessing look. Jilly didn't sound right. With breasts plump enough to fill his hands and a curvy ass that had the bulk of his blood firing straight to his dick, she deserved a far more sensual name.

"I'd just assumed with your new jo—"

Brendan glanced back at Mike. "My what?"

Mike's gaze clouded over. After a few seconds, his grin returned—a little too deviously, in Brendan's mind. Mike used to grin like that back in college, just before he pulled the kind of shit that ended up getting both of them in trouble.

"Never mind what I was about to say." Mike pushed his chair back from the table. "Let me do the honors of introducing you."

Brendan pushed back his own chair and stood. The blonde might not be eyeing him over the way he felt various other women doing, but that didn't mean he needed Mike's help in getting her to talk to him. There was a reason he'd earned the title of "The Midwest's Most Eligible Bachelor" from *People* magazine. That reason wasn't due to shyness around women, knockouts or otherwise. It was because of his money and heritage and, more than that, his business savvy. He'd opted to take a break from the financial aspects of business and try his hand at the advertising end of things less than two years ago. Already he was rising up the corporate ladder with relative ease.

"Thanks for the offer," he said to Mike, "but I can handle things from here."

"Sure thing. Just let me know when you need help."

Brendan laughed at the absurdity of the statement. They might share a passion, and even wisdom, for success, but they sure as hell didn't for females. Mike's knowledge of women could fit into a thimble. If it hadn't been for Brendan literally pushing him in his new wife's direction, the man would still be single.

Single, free and happy.

Guilt edged through Brendan, quickly fading when he noted the nauseatingly doting smile Mike shot his bride's way. Nothing to feel guilty about there, just as there was nothing to be learned. "The day I need help with women from you, Donovan, is the day I'll have truly sunk to an all-new low."

Mike glanced back at him, humor lighting his eyes. "Hey, whatever you say, man. Just remember you said that come Monday."

What was Monday? The day he started in on his latest career venture with the high-power, Atlanta-based advertising firm Neilson & Sons, but what did that have to do with the she-devil working her magic on the dance floor?

Whatever it was, it wasn't important enough to stay in his mind and, therefore, not important enough to worry over.

With a last look at Mike, whose attention was again on his wife, Brendan started across the room. He stopped on the edge of the light-brightened dance floor where a mass of females and a handful of males worked their bodies in a number of interesting moves. None quite so interesting as Jilly's, however.

Her profile was to Brendan, but he could still make out far more than he'd been able to back at the table. Honey-blond hair framed an expressive face and hung midway down her back in loose waves. Full breasts pressed against the snug bodice of her short, sequined dress as her nicely rounded ass swayed seductively in time with the music. Black high-heels streamlined long, slender legs encased in sheer stockings. While her eyes were closed, the sultry look on her face said plenty.

So did the arousal in his tuxedo pants that turned his cock from slightly hard with simple interest to rock-solid and throbbing.

There was something about her. Something he needed to discover before this night was over, or, at the very least, something he needed to uncover by way of removing the layers of silk, sequins and nylon that hid the lush body beneath.

Not about to stand by and wait for her to open her eyes, Brendan moved onto the dance floor and through a sea of thriving bodies to the one he ached to touch.

Jillian Lowery's pulse went from a happily fast beat to all-out chaos in two seconds flat. A hand settled over her belly—a hand that she didn't need to look down at to know was large and masculine. If the sudden throbbing between her thighs that came with the hot breath caressing her neck and the languorous movements against her backside were any sign, the owner of that hand knew exactly what he was doing.

She should stop his highly suggestive and far too intimate moves, whoever he was. Any other day she would. Today wasn't a normal day. Today was the first time in a very long while that she wasn't surrounded by colleagues and clients alike who'd come to respect her cool, professional demeanor. Today the subdued wilder side of Jillian had a chance to come out and play. After today, that Jillian would have to go back into hiding until some unknown time in the future.

She should stop him, but she wasn't going to. Not yet anyway.

Summoning nerves she'd forgotten she possessed, Jillian covered the stranger's hand with her own and ground her bottom against her dance partner's groin. The hand tightened at her waist and a low growl drifted to her ears. The animalistic sound would have been enough to bring too-long-denied hunger swelling to life. The length of an erection pressed against her buttocks was more than enough. Wetness gathered in her panties and her pulse threatened to beat out of control.

The hand beneath hers slid lower, down the sequined silk of her dress, and his palm turned and molded itself to the slight curve of her mound. The breath snagged in her throat. Perspiration gathered on her flushed skin. Her hips reacted out of instinct, grinding against that hot, weighty touch.

Restlessness screamed through Jillian, further moistening her panties with the juices of arousal, making her want in a way she hadn't experienced in years. Maybe ever.

Need egged her on, shut out all thoughts of their surroundings, of the flashing lights and thundering music. Jillian tightened her hold on his hand, urging it to press harder, silently begging him to go farther. To push her dress aside and sink his fingers deep into her aching pussy, thrusting them in and out until she cruised past the limits of ecstasy and there could be no stopping her mindless screams of release.

He pressed the slightest bit harder. Her clit throbbed. She mewled deep in her throat. "Oh, yes. God, please . . ."

She wanted so badly.

Wanted to forget about being the consummate businesswoman. Wanted to let go and be the fun-loving, carefree woman she'd left behind four years ago. Wanted to experience satisfaction once this decade that didn't have anything to do with landing another prestigious client en route to obtaining her dream job.

"I'd love to please you, Jilly, but we're on a dance floor, sweetheart. As crowded as it is, the song's going to end soon and everyone's going to see where my hand's at."

The thickly spoken words drifted to her ears, reflecting appetite as well as humor. Jillian heard both, but it was the truth that pulled her from the sensual haze, the truth of how much she'd allowed herself to forget the mistakes of the past and let herself go. Panic assailed her, tightening her limbs and tamping back the raw desire coiled to life in her belly and burning like a wildfire of need deep in her core. Her grinding moves came to an abrupt halt as judgment returned to taunt her.

Oh, God, what the hell had she been thinking?

She had to stop this. Had to explain that she'd allowed the music to carry her away and act completely shameless with a man she had yet to set eyes on.

But how?

And did she honestly want to?

Anxiety ate at her, but so did the scintillating thrill of doing the kind of daring thing she hadn't done in years. The kind of thing she would never do with or around those who knew her as Jillian the Professional.

The magical hand that had spun warmth and wetness in her with barely more than a touch lifted away. The discontented whimper that broke from her lips answered her earlier question. She didn't want to end this. Only, judging by the fact that her dance partner had let her go, he did.

Dejection filled her for one gloomy second, and then he caught her hand in his and twirled her. She landed awkwardly against a wide, hard chest and swallowed back a breath of mixed shock and elation. He wasn't dismissing her, just changing course as the music dictated.

The flashing overhead lights gave way to the soft glow of candles arranged throughout the reception hall. A slow melody drifted from the front of the room, a mesmerizing song that had nothing on the gripping heat in the stranger's eyes.

They were dark—maybe brown or deep blue; Jillian couldn't tell in the dim lighting. She could tell other things, like his build. He had a good six inches on her five-foot-seven frame, and, if the feel of his body against hers was any sign, he was both muscular and lean. Thick, dark hair framed an angular face that sported a touch of five-o'clock shadow. Full lips hovered over hers as if they might advance at any moment.

Her mind cleared with that last thought and a fresh dose of heat coursed through her. He was yummy, but he was also vaguely familiar. From the wedding party, yes, but for some other reason. Some reason she prayed had nothing to do with business.

"You're a friend of Mike's?" she asked.

He twined her arms around his neck, then placed his own at her waist as they fell into a slow dance. A lazy smile tugged at his lips. "From college, yes."

He was educated, whoever he was. Not that education mattered for what she wanted to do with him, but . . .

What she wanted to do with him? What did she want to do? Okay, have a night of wild and kinky sex—that much was a given, from the shockingly hard points of her nipples to the cream that seeped between her thighs—but did she dare? Not without a little more information.

Jillian didn't want to know him well, just as she didn't want him to know her well. Too much information could lead to potential future problems. A few details were important, though. For starters, if he was married.

But, no, he wasn't married. Mike might only know Jillian through his new wife, Molly, but he still wouldn't allow a married man to come on to her. "What would Mike say if I asked about you?"

The stranger's smile kicked higher. His fingers began a rhythm at her waist that was both featherlight and amazingly distracting. "That I love a good challenge and know how to leave a woman with a smile."

The cockiness of the answer probably should have made her have second thoughts. Instead, she laughed and smiled back. God, how she missed bantering for the hell of it. "So, you're a womanizer?"

"Is that what it sounded like?"

"Is that how it is?"

Seconds ticked by, and Jillion anxiously waited for his response. It came in actions instead of words. His fingers moved higher, along her thinly clothed sides, to graze the outer swell of her breasts. He applied the slightest bit of pressure and her nipples pulsed for his touch.

That dangerously sexy mouth of his curved once more. His eyes showed amusement that ensured he knew the effect he was having on her. It was tempting to turn away and reject him and the arrogance he gave off as far as his sexual appeal was concerned. She might have, too, if at that moment his thumb didn't reach out to stroke the underside of her breast, the pad moving in a leisurely circle that had every one of her nerves at attention.

She bit back a sigh that he would move inward, closer to her straining nipple. There was no need to sigh, no need to beg. She could feel his swollen cock cradled against her belly. He wanted her. All she had to do was say she wanted him, too, and they would be out of there and in some place far more private.

Heat speared through her with the thought of how quickly they could be away from there, their clothes stripped away, limbs tangled, naked and sweaty. Those strong, very capable-looking lips of his on hers, his tongue stroking her flesh with damp, lazy licks. The hot, hard length of his shaft pushing between her thighs and deep into her sheath.

Oh, yes, she wanted that. Wanted to let go and just feel.

If only the circumstances were right. . . .

Jillian struggled to mask her eagerness. That he knew Mike didn't bother her. Once they returned from their honeymoon, Mike and Molly would be moving halfway across the country. The only things that mattered here were that she wouldn't be seeing or hearing from this man after tonight and that her actions with him couldn't return to harm her. "Where are you from?"

The slow movement of his thumb along the underside of her breast paused, starting again with his reply. "Chicago."

Anticipation jetted through her, pushing her building desire to new heights. He wasn't from around here, and the more she looked at him, the more certain she was they'd never met. Those two factors combined were an even greater stimulant than his potent grin. They meant the circumstances were right. And that meant she was going to have the one thing she'd craved these last four years even more than the loud, slightly tacky outfits that used to make up her wardrobe.

She was going to have no-holds-barred, *kill the composure and give into the thrill* sex. Hallelujah!

"What about a name?"

She didn't bother to mask her eagerness and he clearly took note. His penis jerked against her belly and his expression became one of urgency. "Brendan," he said, the calm tone belying his hot look.

"Just Brendan?"

"That would all depend. Is it just Jilly?"

Jillian managed to stop herself from correcting his usage of her childhood name. It was immature and completely removed from the capable, commanding woman she'd transformed herself into. But, for tonight, it was perfect.

Smiling, she moved her hands from his neck to coast over his sides. She thanked the glasses of wine she'd had with dinner, and moved her hands lower still. Her fingers reached his tuxedo pants and, through the thin material of his dress shirt, she caressed the virile flesh just above his waist.

His breath rushed in and his cock jerked once again.

Her smile growing with the distinctly female power that assailed her, she brought her lips to his ear. The spicy tang of aftershave and something far more intoxicating filled her senses as she whispered, "Just Jilly, and so you don't have to waste your time asking, the answer is yes."